D0936016

# Sweet Surrender, Baby Surprise

# KATE CARLISLE

First published in Great Britain 2011
by Mills & Boon, an imprint of Harlequin (UK) Limited,
Large Print edition 2011
Eton House, 18-24 Paradise Road,
Richmond, Surrey TW9 1SR

© Kathleen Beaver 2010

ISBN: 978 0 263 22370 5

Harlequin (UK) policy is to use papers that are natural,
renewable and recyclable products and made from
wood grown in sustainable forests. The logging
and manufacturing process conform to the legal
environmental regulations of the country of origin.

Printed and bound in Great Britain
by CPI Antony Rowe, Chippenham, Wiltshire

# KATE CARLISLE

*New York Times* bestselling author Kate Carlisle was born and raised by the beach in Southern California. After more than twenty years in television production, Kate turned to writing the types of mysteries and romance novels she always loved to read. She still lives by the beach in Southern California with her husband, and when they're not taking long walks in the sand or cooking or reading or painting or taking bookbinding classes or trying to learn a new language, they're traveling the world, visiting family and friends in the strangest places. Kate loves to hear from readers. Visit her website at www.katecarlisle.com.

To the wonderful Susan Mallery,
with love and thanks
for being a true and generous friend.
Drinks are on me!

# One

All Cameron Duke wanted to do was rip off his tie, grab a beer and get laid, not necessarily in that order. He'd been working too hard for way too long on the current Duke Development project and he was damn tired of living in a hotel suite.

On the other hand, he reasoned as he slid his key card into the door slot, he couldn't really complain about it. After all, he owned the hotel. And the owner's suite of the Monarch Dunes resort hotel was two thousand square feet of luxury: all the comforts of home with a wide terrace, fantastic ocean views and room service. Nope, he couldn't complain about that.

As he stepped inside the foyer of his suite, Cameron vowed that as soon as the hotel's international catering conference was over, he would go fishing. The resort was up and running to capacity, so it was time for him to take off for a few weeks, get away and do nothing. Maybe he'd rent a houseboat up on Lake Shasta, or grab a raft and float down the King River. Or maybe he'd just make a few calls….

Not to put too fine a point on it, he definitely needed to get laid.

Pulling his tie loose, he dropped his keys on the foyer side table, placed his briefcase on the marble floor and stepped into the living room, where every light in the room was turned on.

"Now, what's wrong with this picture?" he muttered, knowing he'd switched the lights off when he left two days ago.

Not only was every light on in the suite, but the drapes were all closed. Housekeeping knew he preferred the drapes to stay open in order to take advantage of the incredible Pacific view. The room was on the top floor of the Craftsman-style hotel, and the double-paned windows were tempered glass and lightly tinted. It wasn't as if anyone could see inside.

He shrugged out of his suit jacket. Maybe there was someone new working in Housekeeping. They must've left the lights on and closed the drapes without knowing his preferences. It could happen. But it wouldn't happen again.

Taking a few steps into the room, he saw a strange paperback book, opened and facedown on the coffee table. Then his gaze focused in on another foreign object draped over the arm of the couch.

Moving closer, he carefully picked up the soft bit of fabric. Pink, trimmed with paler pink lace around the edges. Lingerie. Expensive. Absurdly feminine. He fingered the fancy silk and the lightest scent of orange blossoms and spice wafted up and enveloped him. The fragrance was vaguely familiar and his groin tightened as an inexplicable need arose in the pit of his stomach.

"What the hell?" He tossed the camisole back on the couch. Not that he didn't appreciate a nice bit of feminine adornment as much as the next guy, but right now he was more concerned with how in the world it got in here.

"Beer first," he decided, and cut through the spacious dining room to get to the kitchen. That's when he saw the high heels. Sexy ones. Red. Tucked under the dining room table.

He hated to repeat himself, but *what the hell?*

Red high heels? It had to be a joke. Something like this was right up his brother Brandon's alley. And if Cameron hadn't already been annoyed at having his quiet evening interrupted, he might've managed to laugh about it.

He moved cautiously past the bar into the kitchen. No, Brandon wasn't hiding there, waiting to jump out and yell that Cameron had been *Punk'd.* But that didn't mean his brother wasn't around somewhere. Cameron grabbed a beer from the refrigerator, twisted the cap off, took a long, slow drink, then stared at the row of empty baby bottles lined up next to the sink.

Baby bottles?

"Okay, that's enough," he said, then shouted, "Brandon? Where are you?" There was no answer.

"I know you're in here somewhere," he said as he walked through the double doors and down the wide hall toward the master bedroom.

That's when he heard the singing.

He froze. A woman's voice, slightly off key, singing some old song about piña coladas and getting caught in the rain. Some woman was singing in the shower. His shower. In his bathroom.

He glanced at his navy polo shirt neatly tossed over the back of the chair in the corner. Those were his running shoes tucked under the chair, too.

Good. He was in the right suite. Which meant that some woman was definitely in the wrong one. Cameron swore under his breath. This had to be Brandon's work. It would be just like his brother to hire a woman as a "surprise." It was the only explanation, because without the approval of a family member, there was no way the front desk would ever allow a strange woman into his room.

He stood listening to the soft singing and wondered what his next step ought to be. He should probably be a gentleman and wait for whomever it was to finish her shower, dry off and put some clothes on before he kicked her out. But then, he'd never claimed to be a gentleman.

Besides, he wasn't the one guilty of breaking and entering. And showering. So he stood at the entrance to the bathroom and waited as the water was turned off and the shower door opened.

One incredibly shapely, bare, wet leg emerged at the same time as a well-toned, lightly freckled arm reached to grab a towel. Cameron pulled one off the rack and handed it to her. "Allow me."

Her scream was shrill enough to peel the paint off the bathroom wall.

"Get out!" she cried, then dropped the towel in her anxious rush to cover herself up.

"Funny, that's just what I was about to say to you," he told her.

Cameron wasn't normally a voyeur. He should've moved away from the door immediately and given her some privacy, but he couldn't. All he could do was gawk like a school kid at her wet-dream-inducing breasts. High, round orbs with tight pink nipples that he imagined would fit perfectly in his hands. And his mouth. His imagination didn't stop there. He wanted to reach out and touch the smooth skin of her stomach, then let his fingers wander down to the delicious patch of dark blond hair at the apex of her curvaceous thighs.

A spark of light drew his gaze back to her navel, where a small diamond twinkled. She had a pierced belly button. For some reason, that made him smile.

"Will you stop staring and get out of here?" she shrieked as she grappled with the towel, finally covering up those spectacular breasts of hers.

*Show's over,* his rampant libido thought mournfully, and he brought his gaze back up to her face. Whoa. He would know those flashing dark blue eyes anywhere. They belonged to the one woman he'd never quite been able to get out of his mind.

"Hello, Julia," he said.

"What do you think you're doing here, Cameron?"

He leaned back against the doorjamb. "Well, since I live here, I was thinking I'd throw some shorts on, have another beer and watch the football game." He folded his arms across his chest. "A better question might be, what are *you* doing here?"

She huffed out a breath as she stepped fully out of the shower, the towel wrapped around her like a terry-cloth shield. "I was told this suite would be unoccupied for the next two weeks."

"I seriously doubt anyone on my staff told you that."

"Well, it's true," she grumbled, then walked

into the bedroom and over to a small open suit-case on the luggage rack near the window.

He took a sip of beer as he watched her pull out some clothes. "Maybe when you're dressed, we should have a little talk about boundaries."

"Oh, stuff it," she said irately, but her hands shook as she pushed her wet, wavy hair back off her face. "Why are you here, anyway?"

"Me?" He probably shouldn't be smiling still, but after all, he was just a man, and she was gorgeous. "Last time I checked, this was my suite."

"But you're not supposed to be here!"

"Honey, I own the place."

Gripping her towel together with one hand, she pushed past him to the walk-in closet to dress quickly. She emerged less than a minute later, dressed in loose shorts and a T-shirt.

Cameron swore under his breath. If she thought putting on clothes would decrease his desire to stare at her, she was wrong. The small, thin shirt outlined her breasts vividly and Cameron was even more intrigued now than before.

"So, you ready to explain what you're doing

here?" he asked, wondering if it was getting hotter in here.

Fluffing her hair with her fingers to dry it, she began in a calm voice, "Look, Cameron, Sally said that—"

"What?" Every nerve ending in Cameron's body began to twitch and not in a good way. "Wait a minute."

Hearing her invoke his mother's name was not a good thing. Sally Duke, the incredible woman who had adopted him when he was eight years old, was a force of nature. Cameron was well aware of her mission to get her three sons married off and knew she wouldn't be satisfied until the deed was done. Damn it, if Sally had something to do with Julia being here, Cameron was in for nothing but trouble.

"Exactly what does my mother have to do with you being wet and naked in my bathroom?"

Julia gazed at him warily, seeming to gauge his temper. "Um, absolutely nothing. I misspoke."

"You *misspoke?*" he drawled. "About my mother? You're kidding, right?"

"No, I'm not kidding," she said, and straightened her spine in righteous anger. Which caused her breasts to thrust forward. Her wet hair had dampened the T-shirt enough that it molded even more firmly to her skin. But she didn't seem to notice as she persisted. "You're not supposed to be here. And since I was given a key by your hotel management, I think it's only right that you should leave."

"Trust me, that's not going to happen." He prowled toward her, studying her every move. "Now exactly what did my mother tell you?"

Her eyes widened and she took a step back. "Never mind. On second thought, I think I'll just pack my things and get out."

"Not yet," he said, grabbing her arm. "I want to know what my mother has to do with you being here."

"All right," she said as she tried futilely to pull away. "Sally said you'd be gone during the conference and that I would be more comfortable in a suite than a regular room. She told your manager to give me the key."

Her words sent icy tendrils of pure dread down Cameron's spine. Yes, he'd originally planned to stay up north another two weeks, but he'd called Sally yesterday to tell her his plans had changed and he was coming back tonight.

His mother had set this whole thing up.

Did Sally really think that Cameron would take one look at this woman, fall on his knees and beg her to marry him? If so, then Mom was doomed for disappointment.

But as Julia squirmed to pull away from him, Cameron's lower body came to life in a big way. Did it really matter, in that moment, what his mother had done? No. He'd deal with Mom later. Much later.

Right now he had his hands on a lovely, skimpily dressed woman. A sexy woman he'd once known in the most intimate way a man could know a woman.

Holding her close, he again caught that intriguing fragrance of orange blossoms along with something deeper, something exotic. He'd never forgotten her, never forgotten her scent, despite his every effort to do so.

He could still remember meeting her that first time. Talk about lust at first sight.

It all happened after his mother had discovered Cupcake, Julia's bakery in Old Town Dunsmuir. Mom had tried her pastries and cupcakes and had insisted that her sons try them for themselves. They all agreed that her products were incredible and soon thereafter, the Duke resorts began carrying Julia's line of pastries, cookies and breads.

Julia had been invited to attend a one-day vendor orientation at one of the Duke resorts up the coast. She'd planned to stay through the long weekend as a guest of the Dukes. That was where Cameron first saw her, walking across the lobby on her way to the hotel lounge. He'd approached, she'd shown equal interest, and they'd ended up spending that long weekend together.

And that had been the end of it.

She'd haunted his dreams on more than one occasion, but Cameron had refused to contact her again. He had a steadfast rule when it came to women. Once the affair was over, he always made a clean break. He never went back, never looked back. It was safer that way, and simpler. For both parties. Otherwise, women tended to get the wrong idea and hold out hope of a relationship growing. Cameron didn't want to hurt anyone so he stuck to short-term affairs with women who knew the score.

He remembered receiving a few emails from Julia, asking him to call her. He'd thought about it, wanted to, but personal experience had taught him that renewing the affair would only lead to disaster. For her sake as well as his own, Cameron had ignored her requests and eventually, she stopped contacting him.

But here she was, he thought, a year and a half later. In his hotel suite. Wearing those sexy shorts and a practically see-through top. And a belly ring. She gazed up at him with her startling blue eyes and in that moment, he wanted nothing more than to watch those eyes go dark with passion, to taste her lush lips again as well as every other part of her stunning body. Was he honestly going to kick her out of his suite?

Was he nuts?

"Look, I'm sorry," he said in a soothing tone as he ran his hands up and down her arms. "My people must've forgotten I was coming home today. It's late. We can both stay here tonight and I'll find you a room in the morning."

Her eyes clouded with worry. "I suppose I could sleep on the couch."

"We can talk about sleeping arrangements later," he said easily, moving closer. "It's great to see you, Julia."

Smiling tentatively, she said, "Really?"

He skimmed his lips along her hairline and breathed in her fresh scent. "Yeah."

She sighed and closed her eyes, clearly swayed. "But what about your rule?"

Watching her closely, he lowered his head toward hers. "What rule is that?"

Her eyes fluttered open as she whispered, "Once you've finished with a woman, you never go back."

Cameron frowned. "I told you that?"

Nodding solemnly, she said, "It was the last time I saw you. You said you had a great time but you wouldn't call. You said you didn't want me to get the wrong idea." Her voice quavered as his lips hovered within millimeters of hers.

"I'm an idiot," he said, cupping the nape of her neck in his hand.

With a smile, she gazed into his eyes. "You said it's a long-standing rule of yours."

"Rules are made to be broken," he murmured, and covered her mouth with his.

A soft moan escaped her throat as she melted against him. He used his tongue to urge her to open for him and she relented. He thrust into her warmth and felt as though he'd come home. The problems of his world faded and all that mattered was her taste and his need for more.

Wrapping her arms around his neck, she pressed herself even closer. Sweet, was all he could think. Sweet and warm and passionate. He'd missed her, he realized. He shoved that thought away as her tongue teased and tangled with his.

He heard whimpering and wanted to hear more. Wanted to hear her shout his name. Wanted to hear her begging, demanding, crying out for…

*Crying?*

Cameron stiffened. Yes, that was definitely the sound of someone crying somewhere. Outside? Next door? That was odd, since it was almost impossible to hear anything going on outside the suite. The walls of all the rooms were reinforced and soundproofed.

But there it was again, muffled but discernible. He eased back a few inches to make eye contact with her. "Did you hear that?"

"Yes, I did," Julia said, pushing him away and glancing around. Her eyes were sharp as she seemed to be waiting for it to happen again. But there was nothing, and after a moment, Cameron pulled her back into his arms.

"Must've been next door," he whispered, then proceeded to plant soft kisses on her lips, across her cheek, grazing her ear before moving to taste her sexy neck.

She groaned as Cameron maneuvered his hands down her back until he gripped her supple bottom. He pressed his rigid length against her as his mouth devoured hers, then began to guide her toward the bed. He was hot, hard and ready for her.

"Oh, Cameron," she whispered.

"Yeah, baby, I know." He sat on the edge of the bed and eased her closer until she was standing between his legs. He reached for the hem of her T-shirt and began to pull it up, just as a sudden, wailing scream filled the hotel suite.

Julia moaned loudly as she eased out of Cameron's arms. A million and one thoughts raced through her mind all at once. First, the baby needed attention. She'd foolishly left the baby monitor in the master bathroom when she was so rudely interrupted by Cameron, but she knew that if little Jake was fussy, she'd hear him from anywhere in the suite. After that initial scream for attention, he was quiet, but experience had taught her that he wouldn't remain so for long.

Her other million thoughts were all centered around the realization that Cameron would finally meet Jake. She knew it would've happened eventually, but since he hadn't brought up the subject tonight, she was fairly certain that Cameron, stubborn to the end, had never looked at her emails and therefore, had no idea about the baby. Well, she really hoped he liked surprises.

She headed down the hall toward the bedroom door to face the inevitable. "I'd better take care of this."

"Take care of what?" Cameron asked, coming up behind her and wrapping his arms around her waist.

"The noise you heard before? The crying?"

"The noise from next door? I don't hear it now," he said, and continued his sensual onslaught by kissing her neck, then nibbling that most sensitive spot behind her ear.

She couldn't help but sigh deeply. Her skin tingled everywhere Cameron's amazing lips touched her. As his hands worked their magic over her body, Julia recalled that everything about Cameron Duke excited and delighted her.

But why in the world had she trusted Cameron's staff when they'd promised he would be away this whole time? But even his mother had insisted it was safe to stay in the suite. Julia should've known by the twinkle in the older woman's eye when she insisted that Julia stay in Cameron's suite, that she was being set up.

Her first instinct had been to leave Jake at home with the nanny while she traveled to the conference. But their nanny had a chance to go on a cruise with her daughter, and many of Julia's old friends attending the conference were bringing their families with them. They'd all wanted to see little Jake. For that reason, plus the fact that she missed her baby when he wasn't with her, Julia had decided to bring Jake along, too.

It figured that Cameron would cause all her

plans to go awry. It wasn't as if she *never* wanted him to see the baby, but there was no getting around the fact that this was going to get very awkward, very quickly.

"Mmm, that feels so good," Julia murmured as she turned in Cameron's arms and kissed him with all the ardor she could muster. It wasn't a hardship. The man was incredibly sexy and handsome as sin. He seemed taller than she remembered, and definitely stronger. More confident, too, if that were possible. His dark green eyes watched her with a predator's gleam. She shouldn't have found it so absolutely thrilling, but she did.

But damn him for showing up like this! It was just her bad luck, which was the only kind of luck she'd ever had when it came to Cameron Duke.

She'd met him eighteen months ago and willingly succumbed to his charms. They'd had an incredible, torrid four-day affair. Weeks later, she realized she was pregnant.

She'd tried to do the right thing and contact

him, but Cameron had all these damn rules about women. Sure enough, true to his word, he never looked back, never contacted her again.

She'd tried emailing him a few times, but it was sadly obvious now, he'd never read any of her messages. And maybe it was just as well. With his so-called rules regarding relationships—or rather, the obsessive need to avoid them—she'd come to the realization that Cameron Duke wouldn't want to have anything to do with raising a child.

She could just imagine what he would think of her for bringing the baby here, especially when he found out Jake was his. Cameron was a decent man so it wasn't as if he would toss her and Jake out of his suite. But he might accuse her of setting this whole thing up and there was little doubt that he would deny the baby was his.

"Oh," she whispered as he pressed himself closer to her. It was getting impossible to think straight with the delicious onslaught of his mouth and hands, but Julia was starting to wonder if she might possibly distract him long enough to get Jake settled. Then she could deal with everything tomorrow morning. Perhaps it was cowardly, but she could live with that.

Whatever she did would have to happen fast, before her baby decided to take matters into his own chubby baby hands.

"Look, Cameron," she said, finally catching her breath. She needed to get him out of the hallway, now. "Why don't you go get a fresh beer and I'll just slip into something more—"

"I don't need a beer, Julia," Cameron said, running his hands down her sensitive thighs. "I just need this."

"Mmm, me, too," she said as she moved her fingers along his tight, muscled shoulders. "But first, I need a minute to freshen up."

"You took a shower ten minutes ago," he reminded her as he nuzzled her neck. "You're fresh as a daisy."

She moaned, then reluctantly wriggled out of his grasp. "But I really need to dry my hair."

"Yeah?" He brushed a few curling strands away from her face. "It looks fine to me."

"Thanks, but I don't want to catch a cold."

He looked at her skeptically. "Right."

She smiled brightly. "So how's that fresh beer sounding?"

"What?"

"Beer," she repeated. "In the kitchen. And didn't you say you wanted to watch the football game?"

"Yeah, sure. But—"

"Go ahead, then. I'll be right there." She tried to push him toward the living room but the guy was like a brick wall. Unmovable.

"What's going on here, Julia?"

Just then, Jake cried out, "Mama, Mama!"

Cameron's eyes widened.

So much for distractions. She could tell from the tone of Jake's cry that he wasn't hurt or hungry, but that didn't make this moment any easier. "Fine. Look, I didn't want to have to—"

"Okay, I definitely heard that," Cameron said, ignoring her words as he stepped around her handily. "I think it came from the other bedroom."

"No, no, no." Julia jogged just as quickly around to stop him. "It's probably just a cat. I'll take care of it."

"A cat?" Cameron frowned as he glanced down the hall again. "I don't think so."

The baby cried out again and Julia sagged against the hallway wall.

"Aha!" Cameron said and walked toward the second bedroom.

She dashed in front of him and blocked the door. "This is none of your concern, Cameron. Why don't you go turn on the game?"

Cameron was staring at her as if she'd gone insane. Maybe she had. Seeing him again was causing her to behave completely contrary to her usual sensible self. She could blame him for that, too.

"Move it, Julia."

She held up her hand to stop him. "No way. This may be your suite, but you're not going in there without me."

"Then open the door." His look said he wasn't

going anywhere until he'd investigated what he'd heard.

"Fine," Julia said. He'd been bound to find out sometime. The most important thing now was to make sure Cameron didn't upset Jake. She huffed out a breath as she pushed the door open slowly. "But it's not what you think. I mean, it is, but—"

"Oh, really?" he said, stepping into the room and spying the portable crib. Julia followed and saw Jake wearing a great big grin on his face, gripping the railing with both hands as he bounced on the mattress.

"Because I think it's a baby." Cameron turned and glared at her. "What do you think?"

She walked over to the crib, smiled down at her son and whispered, "Looks like a baby to me, too."

Jake's little cheeks were red with exertion and Julia felt a sharp ache in her heart. He held out his arms and his knees began to wobble. "Mama, Mama."

"Hello, my darling." She bent to pick him up

and perched him against her shoulder, rubbing his back. "That's better. Don't worry, sweetie, I'm here. That's my good boy."

"What in the—?" Cameron's tone held a dangerous edge. "Julia, is this your kid?"

She smiled and kissed Jake's soft cheek, inhaled his warm, powdery baby smell, then turned to face Cameron. "Yes, he's mine. And yours. Cameron Duke, I'd like you to meet Jacob Cameron Parrish, your son."

# Two

Cameron immediately stepped back two feet and smacked his elbow into the doorjamb.

"What the hell kind of a joke is this?" he demanded, rubbing his elbow. *Damn, that hurt.* "Trust me, it's not funny."

Apparently, someone disagreed as the baby let out a gut-deep laugh and clapped his hands together. "Ba-da-ba!"

Cameron frowned at the little guy, then glared at Julia, who seemed to be holding back a smile. That set him off even more. He wasn't about to be played for a fool.

He knew the game. This wasn't the first time a woman had tried to pin a paternity suit on him. That was the downside of having a lot of money. The upside was, he wasn't an idiot, despite what he'd told her earlier in jest. He had plenty of lawyers and he knew how to deal with this nonsense. "Not that I believe one word of your story, but the kid's not exactly a newborn. So why'd you wait so long? If he's really mine, why didn't you tell me before now?"

"You're kidding, right?" Julia laughed sardonically. "Cameron, I emailed you a number of times asking you to call me. In the last message I sent, I told you everything. So what part of 'I'm having your baby' didn't you understand?"

His eyes narrowed and he moved in closer. "And what part of 'I don't believe you' do *you* not understand? This is the oldest trick in the book. If you think you're going to get money from me, you're crazy."

"I don't need your money," she said crossly, then lowered her voice as the baby began to fuss. "I was just trying to let you know you were going to be a father. But you couldn't return one lousy email. You couldn't make one stupid phone call. No. You've got *rules*."

She patted the baby to calm him down as she paced the floor in front of the crib. She rounded and came right up to Cameron, clearly riled as she poked him in the chest to emphasize her words. "But you know what? Maybe it's just as well that you ignored Jake and me. With your lifestyle, you probably wouldn't make a very good father anyway."

He grabbed hold of her slender hand before she could take one more poke at him. "Don't you ever insinuate that I would turn my back on my own child."

He dropped her hand and watched her swallow apprehensively. "I didn't. I just meant—"

"I would never hurt my own child," he said through clenched teeth. "I know what it's like to live with a—" Cameron stopped abruptly and raked his hand through his hair. "Hell, never mind."

What was wrong with him? Except for his two

brothers, he'd never told anyone about his childhood. He'd buried it all in the past, right where it belonged. And that ugly childhood was the very reason why he took every precaution to avoid bringing a child into this world. That's why he knew this one couldn't be his.

"I'm sorry," Julia whispered.

Cameron pulled himself together, then turned and said calmly, "Never mind. The fact remains, I don't believe you. We took precautions. I always take precautions."

"Yes, I do, too. But nothing is 100 percent effective." She looked down at the baby in her arms. "Obviously."

"I don't know what game you're playing," Cameron persisted, "but this is not my kid."

"Baba, dada," Jake said, enthusiastically wiggling in his mother's arms. "Dada, ba-boo, dada." He grinned and a tiny dimple appeared in his right cheek.

*Dada?* Cameron frowned and self-consciously scratched his own right cheek, suddenly ill at ease on a whole different level. "Tell him to stop saying that."

Julia laughed. "He's just babbling. It's the first sound babies make. It doesn't mean anything."

Jake kept bobbing and grinning and the little dimple grew deeper. Cameron gritted his teeth. So he happened to have a dimple in his right cheek, too. Didn't mean a thing.

"Come on, sweetie," Julia whispered to the baby, and turned back toward the crib. "Let's see if you'll go back to sleep after all this excitement."

"No! Baba! Dada!" Jake cried, waving his arms and turning to Cameron for help.

"Looks like he wants you to put him to bed," Julia said wryly, and before Cameron could stop her, she thrust the baby into his arms.

"Hey, I'm not—"

"Baba," Jake said, grinning as he bounced in Cameron's arms. "Dada."

Abruptly, the little boy stopped moving and stared meaningfully into Cameron's eyes. Cameron couldn't help but stare back as emotion washed over him. Confusion, affection, anger, frustration, joy, pain. Wonder. Cameron and Jake both blinked, then continued to stare, and Cameron felt as though he were gazing into his own soul. And where had that thought come from? This was just too weird. It couldn't be happening to him. How could he be a father? It was the last thing on earth he ever intended to be.

Jake yawned and closed his eyes. He rested his head on Cameron's chest, his tiny fist gripping Cameron's shirt as though he were claiming ownership. Cameron touched Jake's soft baby hand with his own larger, stronger hand, and felt something shift inside. He tightened his hold around the baby's back, only because the kid might suddenly decide to try for a swan dive if he wasn't careful. That was his story, anyway.

"He's sleepy," Julia said quietly. "Just lay him down on his back and rub his tummy a few times. He'll be fine."

"Sorry, pal, but your mom has spoken," Cameron said in a low tone. He leaned over the crib and laid the baby down on the soft mattress. Cameron ran his hand over Jake's head. The kid's blond hair was impossibly soft.

Jake didn't whimper or balk, but stayed right where he was. He stuck two fingers in his mouth and continued to stare up at Cameron in pure fascination.

Cameron had to admit Jake was a darn good-looking kid, but that didn't make him his son.

Aw, hell. Who was he kidding? One look at the little guy with his shock of golden blond hair and the shape of his dark green eyes, not to mention the dimple in his cheek—though Cameron hated the word dimple, for God's sake—and anyone would see it, plain as daylight. The kid was Cameron Duke's.

Still, he couldn't shake loose the idea that Julia Parrish was playing him for a fool. Who was to say she hadn't gotten herself pregnant on purpose? Everyone knew the Dukes had money, so maybe she was looking for a handout. Cameron would never shirk his duty to his son, but that didn't mean he was going to make it easy for Julia.

As the baby's eyes closed and he began to sleep, Cameron led the way out into the hall. As Julia closed the door to the bedroom, Cameron turned and said sharply, "I'll want a paternity test."

She froze. He could see he'd shaken her. What? Did she expect him to just believe her with no proof? But watching her now, he remembered how her face had always been an open book. He'd known exactly what she wanted by her facial reaction to everything he did to her, everywhere he touched her. She'd been so forthright about how much she enjoyed his touch. Did she have a dishonest bone in her body? he wondered.

Of course she did. Most of the women he'd dated did.

"Fine," she said grudgingly. "We'll do a paternity test."

Cameron's mind jolted back to the present. "Okay. Good. I can get it done tomorrow."

"I start my conference tomorrow," she said,

leading the way into the living room. Cameron watched her backside move with a graceful, long-legged sexiness. He remembered that, too.

She picked up the book she'd left on the coffee table and turned. "I won't be able to take the baby to the doctor until I get back to town."

"Wait a minute," Cameron said, her words sinking in. "You're here for the conference?"

She looked at him like he'd grown another head. "Of course I'm here for the conference. Why else would I be staying here in your hotel room?"

*To seduce me into paying child support,* Cameron thought, but didn't say it aloud. He wasn't a fool. Sometimes he needed to remind himself of that fact. He coughed to cover his hesitation. "We have a nurse on call at all times. I'll have her come by the room tomorrow to draw blood."

"Okay." Julia shivered visibly and rubbed her arms.

"What's wrong?"

She sighed. "I know it's necessary, but I hate the idea of Jake having his blood drawn."

"It's important," he said, then tried not to cringe himself at the thought of that needle going into Jake's arm. Cameron was already having second thoughts. He'd only insisted on the paternity test to punish Julia, but she wouldn't be the one getting stuck in the arm with a needle. No, that would be Jake, who seemed way too small to have to deal with stuff like that.

Who was Cameron kidding? Jake was his child. The blood test wouldn't be necessary.

He wasn't happy about the way Julia had sprung the news on him, but he believed her. He wouldn't tell her tonight, though. Better to let her squirm for a few hours. He'd tell her in the morning after he'd had a few strong shots of caffeine.

"Fine." Julia swiped the sexy camisole off the chair cushion and grabbed her high heels from under the dining room table. Then she headed into the kitchen and began gathering the baby bottles on the sink.

"What are you doing?" he asked.

"I've got to pack our things."

"Wait." Cameron grabbed hold of her arm before she could go any farther. "No packing. You're staying here."

She looked up at him. "We can't stay here, Cameron. *You're* here."

"Exactly," he said decisively. "That's why you're staying here, too."

She gave him that big-eyed incredulous look of hers again. Why he found it so sexy, he couldn't say. Maybe he enjoyed the challenge she provided.

Shaking her head, she said, "If you think something's going to happen between us, you're wrong."

"Honey," he drawled. "I think we proved awhile ago that it definitely could happen."

"Now, look—"

"You're right, though," he continued. "It's not going to happen tonight." With a casualness he didn't feel, he let go of her arm and walked into the living room. "But you're still staying here."

"Okay," she said, following him. "I'd rather not disrupt the baby tonight anyway. We'll move to another room in the morning."

An irrational shot of annoyance ran through him and he covered it by grabbing another beer from the refrigerator and popping the top off. "You don't get it, babe. You're staying here until the paternity test is completed. In fact, you might as well stay through the conference. There won't be any rooms available anyway."

She gritted her teeth. "I gave my room away when your mother insisted I stay here. I don't suppose it'd still be available."

"It's not, trust me," he said. "Besides your conference, we've got a golf tournament here this weekend."

She flashed him a frown of frustration. "But you own this place. You should be able to find another room for me and Jake."

"I could, but I'm not going to," he said flatly, then pointed toward the back bedroom. "If that *is* my son in there, I don't want him staying anywhere but here. With me. And we'll know the truth soon enough, won't we?"

"I think that went well," Julia muttered to herself as she slipped between the sheets of the twin bed in the guest room. Jake was sleeping soundly, completely unaware of the drama going on around him. She was gratified to hear his innocent baby snores and wished more than anything that he would never have to be touched by unhappiness of any kind. She knew she couldn't shield him forever, but for now, he didn't need to know that his mommy and daddy were in such an emotional twist over him.

She tried to concentrate on her son, tried to picture his soft little hands waving in the air and hear his funny belly laugh, but visions of Cameron kept interfering. She winced as she remembered how easily she'd melted in his arms. How could he still wield that kind of power over her? She'd known that one day she would have to confront him with the reality of Jake, and she'd steeled herself for that moment. But he'd caught her unprepared. Now he knew how susceptible she was to his charms. He knew he could wiggle his finger and she would come running.

It was humiliating to know that he was right.

In a matter of hours, she would have to tangle with him once more. Would she come running to him again? Or would she be able to withstand his immense allure? It was almost as if he'd put a spell on her.

Yawning, she fluffed her pillow and tried to settle her active mind by breathing deeply for a count of ten. She knew she would need all the sleep she could get if she expected to put up a good fight tomorrow.

Cameron stretched, then tried to turn over onto his back—and landed on the floor.

"What the—?" he grumbled. Where the hell was he?

His brain slowly engaged and he groaned as he remembered exactly where he'd slept last night. Moving slowly, he pulled himself up off the living room floor, then sat on the couch with his elbows resting on his knees.

After Julia had gone off to bed, he'd finished his beer and tried to watch the football game, but it had lost its appeal. So he went to bed where he tossed and turned, unable to sleep with the knowledge that Julia was sleeping in the room just across the hall. He wanted her in bed with him. Wanted her lush body pressed against his. Wanted to bury himself in her silken warmth.

But you can't always get what you want, he thought. Not right away, anyway. He was a patient man and he would have her in his bed soon enough.

Last evening, though, that thought had not been conducive to a good night's sleep. So Cameron had come out to the living room couch, thinking he'd zone out on late-night television. He finally fell asleep and now he regretted it as he stood and tried to stretch out his spine. Damn, his couch looked spacious and luxurious, but spending the night on it had been a tactical error. His back was whimpering like a whiny schoolgirl.

He stood and stretched and tried to remember when, exactly, had he turned into such an old man? He was barely into his thirties.

Determined to work out and get rid of the aches and pains, he slipped on a pair of gym shorts and sneakers, then left the suite for a brisk twenty-minute run around the resort grounds.

Forty-five minutes later, after a hot shower and two cups of coffee, he felt a whole lot better. A good thing, because he would need to be in peak condition to deal with the new occupants of his suite.

"Dada!"

Speaking of.

"Good morning," Julia said as she carried Jake into the room. She had him in some kind of space-age kid carrier and without thinking, Cameron took it from her and placed carrier and baby up on the breakfast bar.

She was dressed in a sleek, navy pinstriped suit with a crisp white blouse and black heels. Her wavy blond hair was tamed back into a simple ponytail. And why he found that look so damn sexy, Cameron couldn't figure out, but he knew he was on a slippery slope, watching her walk around the kitchen as she grabbed an apple for herself and warmed a bottle for the baby.

"Dada," Jake whispered, gazing up at Cameron's face.

"He says that a lot," Cameron said, staring at the kid. He realized as he spoke that Jake's repetition of the word *dada* didn't bother him half as much as it had last night.

"It feels good on his tongue," Julia explained, then blinked and quickly turned toward the coffeemaker.

Cameron laughed as she crisscrossed the kitchen, her cheeks blushed pink after realizing what she'd just said. Obviously, she hadn't thought about the words before uttering them, and now he could think of a few things, too, that would feel good on *his* tongue.

"I've got a conference panel in forty minutes," she said briskly, back to business after a few hurried sips of coffee. "I've arranged for a babysitter to watch Jake for the day, and she should be here any minute. But if you'd rather not have anyone in the suite while you're here, I'll understand. I can check with the concierge for another place to—"

"It's fine if the babysitter stays here."

"Okay." She nodded. "Good. Thanks."

"Did you sleep well?" he asked.

"Wonderful, thank you," she said, and rinsed her coffee mug. "You?"

"Like a rock," he lied.

"That's great."

Well, this was awkward. He leaned against the bar, watching as Julia put the mug in the dishwasher. Then he glanced over at Jake, whose eyes were closed. He was already sleeping peacefully, Cameron realized. Must be nice.

The doorbell rang and Jake's eyes flew open. His mouth quivered in a pout, and Cameron realized he was about to cry.

"Hey, kiddo, it's okay," he said softly, and stroked his tummy. "Shh. Don't worry. Doorbells scare me, too."

Jake stared up at Cameron as though his words

were written on stone tablets. A wave of something powerful swept through him and he felt as if he just might be the most important person in the world in that moment.

"That must be the sitter," Julia said, her voice a little hoarse. "I'll go let her in."

Ten minutes later, the babysitter and Jake were ensconced in the back bedroom, and Julia was ready to leave. She had her purse strapped over her shoulder and she carried a soft leather briefcase. She looked like a lawyer instead of the best pastry chef on the Central Coast. Cameron walked her to the front door and opened it.

"I showed her where everything is and gave her my card in case she needs to call me," Julia said nervously. "I won't turn off my phone."

"Everything will be okay," he said, and leaned against the door jamb, blocking her way out. "Look, we haven't talked about the paternity test yet."

"Oh," she said. With a frown, she dropped her briefcase and folded her arms across her chest.

"I was hoping you'd changed your mind about that."

He narrowed his eyes. "You don't think I'm handing you a child support check until I've verified that Jake is my son, do you?"

"I don't need child support, Cameron," she said testily. "You can keep your money."

"Yeah, that's what they all say."

Her lips thinned in anger. "First of all, it's Jake's comfort I'm concerned about. Do you have any idea how many immunizations he's been through in his short nine months? I've lost track of the number of needles he's had to suffer through. But don't worry, you'll have your damned paternity test. Second of all—"

"Look, Julia, I—"

She held up her hand. "Just let me finish before you say anything else you'll regret later about the money thing. Do yourself a favor, go online on Google and look up the Parrish Trust. When I get back, we'll talk about money."

"Fine." He realized he'd pushed her a little too

far, but where did she get off thinking he'd just accept her word on everything?

She picked up her briefcase and started to walk out, but stopped again and glared at him. "And as long as you've got your computer fired up, you might want to take a look at those emails I sent you a while back. They just might paint a different picture than what you think is going on here."

"Julia, I'm not—"

"And while you're at it," she said, pulling a flowery scrapbook from her briefcase, "I brought this to show some friends, but you might want to take a look at it first."

He stared at the thick journal, then began to thumb through it casually. There were photographs of the baby affixed to the pages, along with handwritten passages describing the pictures. Frowning, he gazed at her.

"And one more thing," she continued before he could say anything. "You caught me in a weak moment last night, but it won't happen again. We're willing to stay here with you for the next ten days, but there's no way I'm having sex with you. That's a deal-breaker."

With that, she left the suite in a huff.

# Three

*That's a deal-breaker.*

Sex? A deal-breaker? Not in this universe, Cameron thought. He could recall Julia melting in his arms last night and knew it was only a matter of time until he had her in his bed.

After she left for the conference, Cameron pulled his computer out of the second bedroom and set everything up in the dining room. That way, he wouldn't disturb Jake when it was nap time later.

Cameron couldn't get Julia's irate words out of his head so, with great reluctance, he finally did as she suggested and went online to research her family business.

Now, he sat back in his desk chair and stared at the computer screen. A thousand different thoughts ran through his mind, but the first thing he did was pick up the phone and call his company's tech department.

After putting in a request that they immediately recover the emails from Julia he'd deleted more than eighteen months ago, Cameron hung up the phone and went back to gazing at the online information he'd pulled up on Julia Parrish and her family.

It was disturbing to read that Julia's parents had died in a small plane crash when she was ten years old. There were pages and pages devoted to her parents' philanthropy, but almost nothing on young Julia Parrish until she opened her popular bakery shop in Old Town Dunsmuir Bay four years ago.

Did she have other family in the area? Who had been responsible for raising her? Cameron found more questions than answers and knew they would have to talk about these and other issues tonight.

Aside from the news of her parents' death, the most shocking fact about Julia Parrish was that the woman was almost as wealthy as Cameron was. So why was she slaving away making cupcakes for other people?

It turned out that the Parrish Trust was one of the biggest and most influential charitable organizations in the state. The trust funded or underwrote everything from children's television to scientific research to humanitarian efforts on behalf of children everywhere. Cameron had heard of the Parrish Trust, of course. Who hadn't? But he'd never connected the dots from the trust to Julia, never had any reason to. Now, though, he had a reason.

No wonder Julia didn't care about Cameron's money. No wonder she'd given up on trying to contact him. She didn't need Cameron Duke's support. The mother of his son was worth millions.

He didn't know how he felt about that. He

supposed it wasn't a bad thing that little Jake would never want for anything in his life. In fact, that was definitely a good thing. But Cameron wanted to be the one to provide those things for his son. And he would. As soon as Julia got back to the suite, they would talk. He would tell her she didn't have to worry anymore about being the sole provider. Cameron was ready and willing to step in and take care of things from now on.

"Oh, that'll fly like a lead balloon," he uttered, then shrugged. Didn't matter what she thought. Cameron was Jake's father and he would be responsible for him. Besides, why shouldn't Julia take a break and let Cameron shoulder some of the burden for a while? It's not like he was forcing her into a marriage. God forbid. Neither of them wanted that.

Although, now that he thought about it, a marriage between Cameron and Julia would be the best thing for Jake.

"But that's never going to happen." He shoved his chair back from the table. If Cameron didn't do relationships, he sure as hell wouldn't ever do marriage. And that was okay. Jake would thrive with two parents who cared about him. They didn't need to be living together in order for the kid to have a good life.

Cameron hadn't exactly grown up with great role models. Quite the contrary, his dad had been a lousy excuse for a parent and a miserable marriage partner to his mom. Cameron had always said that if his parents were what marriage was all about, he wasn't interested.

And if his unhappy parents weren't enough of a reminder that marriage was out of the question for him, there was also the sacred pact he'd made with his brothers. He would never break that pact, ever.

Cameron could still picture the day, shortly after his eighth birthday, when he arrived at Sally Duke's big house on the cliffs of Dunsmuir Bay. At first, it was unsettling to learn that Sally had rescued two other boys from foster care along with Cameron, and that she expected all of them to become a family.

Those early weeks he spent getting to know Adam and Brandon were bumpy, to say the least. A pecking order needed to be established, so the three boys fought for supremacy over everything: toys, food, television shows, Sally's attention. They bickered and clashed just like eight-year-old boys were supposed to. At the same time, they worried that Sally might dump them back on the state coffers. It wouldn't be the first time for any of them. But they didn't know Sally Duke.

One day when she'd heard enough arguing, Sally banished the boys to the custom-designed tree house she'd had built for them. She told them they could come down when they'd learned to behave like friends and brothers.

Cameron, Adam and Brandon spent hours in that tree house, and eventually their worst secrets were unraveled and shared. Brandon's drug-addict mom ran off and his dad used to beat him until the man was killed in a bar fight. Adam's parents abandoned him when he was barely two years old. He was raised in an orphanage before being thrown into the foster care system.

Cameron finally confessed that his own father was a violent man and his mother bore the brunt of it. Not that she was all that loving, given her appetite for alcohol and drugs. Cameron knew she had lied and stolen and worse to support her habit, but he blamed his father for turning her into an addict. He still had nightmares of his mother screaming from the beatings his father inflicted. Even worse, Cameron could never forget hearing his old man hit his mom while yelling that he was doing it because he loved her. And he would never forget waking up and finding them both dead. He was seven years old.

When Adam and Brandon heard that Cameron's dad thought he was showing love by beating the crap out of his mother, they both were disgusted. That led to the pact.

First, the three eight-year-olds swore loyalty to each other. Next, they made a sacred vow that they would never get married and have kids, because it was clear that marriage turned people mean and stupid. Married people hurt each other and their kids.

Finally, they vowed to make Sally Duke proud that she'd chosen them.

From that day forward, Sally let them know in a hundred different ways that they'd fulfilled their third vow—and then some. They'd all grown up to be honorable, successful men and she couldn't be more proud. Of course, now Sally had come up with some cockamamie plan to marry the brothers off so they could give her a bunch of grandkids. And despite all of his diatribes, Cameron had just given her exactly what she wanted.

"Oh, man," he said aloud. The realization had him rubbing his knuckles against his chin. "Wait'll Mom gets a look at little Jake." He chuckled in anticipation of the scene that awaited him when Sally heard the news.

Of course, she might be a little disappointed that he had no intention of marrying Julia, but she would just have to live with it. Cameron would never marry, that was all there was to it.

He would never want to destroy someone else the way his parents had destroyed each other.

It's not like he'd been a martyr to his fate. Cameron had tested the waters more than once, in spite of the boyhood pact. But things had never worked out, to put it mildly. There had been plenty of women in his life and a few attempts at serious relationships, but they'd been disastrous. He'd used those as strong reminders that he'd come from bad stock and things would never change. He wasn't willing to put someone else through that kind of pain, let alone experience it again himself. No, he was meant to go it alone, and that suited him just fine, thanks.

He stood and checked his wristwatch. The babysitter had taken Jake for a long walk around the hotel grounds so Cameron could have a short meeting with his brothers here in the suite. They were due any minute.

They would soon find out they were uncles, Cameron thought. So much for sacred pacts. But at least Cameron hadn't been the first brother to break it. That honor went to Adam when he married Trish James last month.

The doorbell rang and Cameron greeted his brothers, then led the way to the kitchen. "You guys want beers?"

"You have to ask?" Brandon said, swinging the refrigerator door open and grabbing three bottles from the shelf.

"How's Trish?" Cameron asked Adam, knowing his brother had brought his wife along for a quiet, romantic weekend at Monarch Dunes.

"She's great," Adam said with a smile. "She ran into Mom and her friends downstairs so they're probably relaxing at the pool by now."

"Relaxing?" Brandon laughed. "We'd better get this over with so you can rescue her."

"Good idea." Adam sat at the dining room table and opened a thin binder of notes and spreadsheets.

Cameron and Brandon joined him at the table where they discussed some last-minute scheduling items that had arisen over the hand-off of priority projects from the Monarch Dunes resort to the Napa Valley property.

"You've done a great job with Monarch Dunes, bro," Brandon said, tipping his beer bottle in Cameron's direction.

"Thanks," Cameron said. "Napa's looking good, too."

The three men had found out years ago that the best way to run their development company was to put each brother in charge of a particular property from start to finish. The Monarch Dunes property had been Cameron's baby from day one and he'd run the project much as he ran his life: with military precision.

The multifaceted, multileveled Craftsman-style resort, located forty miles south of their home town of Dunsmuir Bay, was already completely booked for the next three seasons and on its way to becoming the premier destination spot along California's Central Coast.

Cameron had had a hand in every decision along the way, from the expansiveness of the lobby that opened to a spacious terrace

overlooking the ocean and cliffs, to the place-
ment of the greens on the state-of-the-art cham-
pionship golf course that wound around the wide
perimeter of the hotel.

"My staff is more than ready to have me
move out of here," Cameron admitted. "They've
started saluting me when I ask them to do something."

"When you *ask* them to do something?" Adam
said sardonically. "More like barking out orders,
I'd say."

Brandon shook his head. "Once a marine,
always a marine."

With a shrug, Cameron said, "Hey, I just prefer
to have things done the right way, so let's get
back to business." He read his notes off a legal
pad. "I'll let my assistant know that the Napa
grand opening will be pushed back one week to
coincide with the grape harvest and crush. She
can coordinate schedules with the Napa staff."

The Dukes' Napa property was being built ad-
jacent to the acres of vineyards and the winery
they'd purchased years ago. The white wines

were already being marketed all over the country and the reds were on the verge of reaching world-class status.

"Good," Brandon said and walked toward the kitchen. "Hey, what's this?"

Too late, Cameron realized Brandon had picked up the scrapbook Julia had given him earlier. "It's nothing. I'll take it."

But Brandon was already thumbing through the pages. "Dude, these are baby pictures. It's a baby album."

"Who's the baby?" Adam asked, moving around the table to see what Brandon was looking at.

*Hell.* Cameron reached for the book. "I'll take that."

"I don't think so," Brandon said and whipped the book away.

Adam pierced Cameron with a look. "Was there something you wanted to share with us?"

"I'm not playing this game." Cameron held out his hand and waited calmly until Brandon gave him the thick scrapbook. "Okay, I'll see you guys later."

"You're kidding, right?" Brandon said, both hands fisted on his hips. He turned to Adam. "I saw a shot of a pregnant woman. And an ultrasound photo."

"So what?" Cameron said. He wasn't about to let his brothers see anything else in the book before he'd had a chance to thoroughly view every page.

"What's going on, Cam?" Adam asked quietly.

Feeling cornered but knowing there was no way out, Cameron sat back down at the table. "Fine. I was going to tell you anyway."

"Well, let's hear it." Brandon pulled out his chair and sat.

"I have a son."

Stunned silence greeted his announcement. Brandon blinked a few times, opened his mouth to speak, but ended up saying nothing.

Adam's eyes narrowed. "Mind repeating that?"

Brandon folded his arms across his chest. "I knew that was an ultrasound."

Cameron glared at Brandon. "No, you didn't."

"Yeah, I did." Brandon lifted his shoulders philosophically. "I'm smarter than I look."

Adam and Cameron both laughed, easing some of the tension in the room.

"I think you owe us some explanation after dropping that bomb," Adam said.

They'd only torment him until he spilled everything, so he gave them the abbreviated story of Julia and baby Jake.

"You never read the rest of her email messages?" Brandon said incredulously. "Weren't you curious? I would be."

"Yeah, well, I've got more control than you," Cameron said, his tone slightly defensive.

"Control *issues,* you mean," Brandon replied.

Adam chuckled. "I think we should check out some of those messages."

"I told you I erased them all," Cameron said, not willing to add that he'd also taken steps to recover them. By now, they were probably waiting in his email in-box.

Adam grabbed Cameron's shoulder and said,

"Maybe so, but you've got the baby book. Let's check it out."

"I don't think so."

"Dude, we're your brothers," Brandon said. "We can add some objectivity to the situation."

He had a point. They both did, as much as Cameron hated to admit it. In fact, it seemed fitting that they were there with him, considering that bits of their sacred brotherhood pact were crumbling to dust by the minute.

Against his better judgment, he opened the book. His brothers pulled their chairs up close to look at the photo on the first page. It was of Jake, taken in the hospital within an hour after he was born.

"He looks like a grizzled old man," Brandon said.

"No, he doesn't," Cameron argued.

Adam sat back. "Babies always look like that. You've got to consider where they just came from."

"Oh, man," Brandon said, flinching. "That's just rude."

Cameron chuckled as he turned the page and gazed at a number of early photos of Jake, some with Julia holding him. He wondered who had been operating the camera. He was dismayed to realize that it should've been him. But he'd completely ignored Julia. It grated on him more and more as he turned the pages and saw his good-looking little boy growing bigger and bigger.

"Oh, man, he's in heaven," Brandon said, as they stared at the shot of Jake enjoying his first barbecued chicken. Julia wrote next to the picture that the chicken had been pureed for Jake and he'd eaten it quickly, but then he'd taken his time enjoying the sauce. Cameron had to laugh. Jake's little face and hair were smeared with red sauce and he flashed the camera a big, toothless grin.

"Looks just like Cameron when he eats barbecue," Adam said, and even Cameron had to laugh at that one.

He turned to another set of pictures. Julia had titled them Jake's First Immunizations and described how the nurse's assistant had taken the pictures while Julia held and comforted the baby.

"Uh-oh, this is gonna hurt," Brandon said, wincing. Cameron did the same. The first photo showed the nice doctor holding a small syringe. Several more shots documented Jake's expressive face as it scrunched up in preparation for something bad to happen. The last picture showed the dam bursting. Jake's face was purple with rage, his eyes were shut tight and his mouth was wide open. He was obviously screaming in terror and pain.

Cameron could almost hear the screams.

"Man, that's just cruel," Adam said, averting his eyes from the book.

"I completely feel his pain," Brandon agreed, rubbing his arm where the needle would've gone in.

The next page showed the look of happy shock on the baby's face as his mother took him into the ocean for the first time. He stared at Julia frolicking in a brief bikini, looking so lush and sexy he had to stifle the urge to stroke the page.

With a start, he realized his brothers could see her as well, and immediately turned the page.

"Hey, wait, not so fast," Adam complained.

"Yeah, slow down," Brandon said. "That photographer is really talented. I want to see more of the ocean."

"Yeah, right," Cameron said, shaking his head. He knew what his brothers wanted to see more of and he wasn't about to give them what they wanted. Nobody was going to look at Julia in a bikini but him. His brothers would have to learn to live with disappointment.

"Come on, Cam, go back to that last shot," Adam said, then added in a reasonable tone, "We really should get to know Jake's mom better."

"You've both seen enough," Cameron said, and closed the book.

"Fine," Brandon said, and sat back in his chair. "But I still wonder why you didn't get in contact with her when you got her messages."

Cameron turned and glared at him. "All I saw in that first message was a woman demanding that I call her. Who needs that? So I deleted the ones she sent after that."

"Seems a little harsh," Brandon replied.

"Oh, come on. You've dealt with obsessed women. What would you have done?"

Brandon frowned but said nothing.

"He has a point," Adam said reluctantly.

Cameron expelled a long, slow breath. "I did what I had to do at the time."

"Yeah, been there," Brandon said with a sigh. He'd spent ten years in the NFL and knew what it was like to be stalked by an obsessed woman or two. Or three. "I guess I can't blame you. But she looks so normal."

"Don't get me wrong," Cameron said. "I liked her a lot. But then the messages started. That first day, she sent four emails. Four. Seriously, she showed all the signs of a desperate woman who'd talked herself into something that wasn't there. Like, we had sex and suddenly she was in love or something, demanding that I call her. She even sent me a letter, but I threw it away unopened. I wasn't willing to buy into any of it."

"I guess I see your point," Adam admitted.

"Thought you might," Cameron said. "Then all of a sudden, the emails stopped coming and I figured she got the message."

"Guess she gave up on you," Brandon said with a shrug.

That didn't sit well with Cameron, but he said nothing.

Adam gazed at him. "So where do you go from here?"

"I'm working it out."

"Yeah?" Brandon chuckled. "Good luck with that."

Cameron's jaw tightened and he shot his brother a scornful look. "I'm in complete control of the situation."

"Ah, the famous Cameron control," Adam said, nodding sagely. "So now she's living here with you for the next ten days or so. I have a feeling your legendary control is going to be tested to the max."

The way Adam chuckled, Cameron imagined he'd had his own share of control issues.

And knowing Trish now, he was pretty sure his brother had already lost that battle. Strangely enough, Adam didn't look like he minded one bit.

Cameron was glad his brother had found happiness, but marriage and a family weren't on Cameron's agenda.

Adam stood and slipped his binder into his briefcase. "Trish is going to want to see the baby."

"Hey, me, too," Brandon said. "I want to meet my nephew."

"How about if we swing by tonight?"

"Tonight's not good," Cameron said quickly. He needed to prepare Julia for the family onslaught. "I'll set something up for tomorrow night."

Ten minutes after his brothers took off, the babysitter returned with Jake. Cameron watched her carefully as she changed the baby's diaper and fed him his bottle. He asked a few pertinent questions and had her show him some of her techniques, then he gritted his teeth and told her she could go for the day. He was ready to take over.

"It's just you and me now, kid," he murmured to Jake after the woman left. Cameron lifted the baby into his arms and spent a few minutes walking Jake around the suite. They stood at the window and stared out at the cliffs and the ocean beyond. Cameron pointed out a few landmarks up and down the coast.

"Can you see that bit of land jutting out into the ocean?" Cameron said, pointing northward. "That's where we live."

A seagull flew high over the ocean and Cameron said, "Can you wave at the bird? Sure, you can. I'll help you." He grabbed Jake's wrist and moved it up and down in a waving gesture.

"Smart boy," he murmured, and breathed in the powdery scent of clean baby.

No, marriage and family hadn't been on Cameron's radar, but now that he had Jake to take care of, he was already mentally planning to do everything he could to contribute to the boy's welfare. Jake would never want for anything as long as Cameron had a breath left in his body.

He was amazed to realize that he'd already developed strong feelings for the little boy. He wouldn't call it love. He wasn't sure he would ever be ready to take that step and say those words. Maybe it would be better for Jake if he never did.

"Dadadada," Jake gibbered.

"Hey, kiddo," Cameron said, and gave him an affectionate squeeze. "Let's see about getting you something to munch on."

They walked into the kitchen where Cameron found some Cheerios for Jake and crackers for himself. He put Jake in his high chair and watched the baby amuse himself with the little O's.

Despite the violence of his early years, Cameron had lucked out when Sally Duke adopted him. Through her strong and loving influence, Cameron learned to trust again. Even though his father had warned him that nobody would ever find him worth a damn, Cameron knew he was capable of giving and accepting love. He'd been with plenty of women all through high school and, even though he couldn't say he'd loved any of them, he'd certainly felt affection for them and knew the feelings were reciprocated.

Then, in his senior year, he met Wendy, a beautiful girl who fell for him, hard. One night, she told him she loved him and demanded that Cameron say it, too. In one of the dumbest moves of his life, he told her he loved her. But he didn't, and soon after that, he tried to break it off as gently as he could. Wendy went wild. She tried everything to force him to take her back, even tried to turn his friends against him. Then she tried blackmail, threatening to tell his teachers that he cheated on his exams. Cameron ignored her, so she finally went to the police and pressed charges, accusing him of abusing her. That was the final straw.

Given his early upbringing, Cameron was the last person who would ever physically abuse anyone. Wendy didn't know that, but Sally Duke did. She circled the wagons and hired a lawyer. In the courtroom, Wendy broke down and admitted she was lying. She recanted the charges, but the damage had been done.

Cameron could still feel the anger and adrenaline that shot through his system as the judge cleared his name. If things had gone the other way, would he have reacted violently, like his father?

In a desperate attempt to channel the fury he knew was inside him, he joined the marines. And he vowed that he would never again give anyone the power to destroy him in the name of love.

But now there was Jake. And there was Julia. What was he supposed to do about them?

Julia finished her food allergies workshop and stayed over to answer all the questions from the audience. Even after she left the meeting room, several of her attendees followed, peppering her with more. This was the part of the conference she loved—glad to pass on the things she'd learned from her own mentors and teachers over the years. She considered it a tribute to her mentors and teachers that she was now able to share the knowledge they'd generously given.

She bid her students goodbye and entered the lobby, then stopped abruptly. Sally Duke stood with two other women by the concierge desk, fifty feet away. They were all dressed casually in Bermuda shorts, colorful T-shirts and walking shoes.

Julia didn't know whether to avoid Cameron's mom or confront her. After all, Sally had to have known Cameron was due back last night, yet when they'd run into each other yesterday, the older woman had blithely assured Julia that Cameron would be out of town for the duration. After all her careful planning, Julia couldn't believe she'd walked right into a trap.

If Julia had known otherwise, she might've thought twice about attending the conference at all. And she definitely would've left Jake with their nanny back in Dunsmuir Bay.

Feeling like the worst kind of coward, Julia

skulked away to avoid another run-in with Cameron's lovely mother. As she scurried down a long hallway toward the bank of elevators at the far end of the hotel, Julia thought back to that moment the day before when she and Jake had first arrived at the resort.

She'd been pushing Jake in his stroller while a bellman followed with a luggage trolley stacked to the top with Julia's suitcases and conference supplies and piles of baby paraphernalia. From across the wide-open lobby, someone had cried out her name.

"Julia, what a delightful surprise!"

She'd been shocked to see Sally Duke standing there when she turned to look. Normally, she would've been happy to see her Dunsmuir Bay friend. After all, Sally Duke had put Julia's bakery on the map when she'd insisted that her sons carry Julia's products in all the Duke resorts.

But before Julia had even been able to say hello, Sally had bent over to take her first look at baby Jake. Julia would never forget her own sense of apprehension as she watched the older woman's reaction to the baby. Would she recognize the strong resemblance to her own son?

Julia had hesitated, then said, "Sally, this is my son, Jake."

"Oh, how wonderful." Sally knelt down in front of the stroller, grabbed hold of Jake's foot and said, "Hello, you little darling. I'm so happy to meet you."

Jake giggled and his dimple popped out on his right cheek. Sally gasped and her mouth dropped open. She stared at the baby for another moment, then looked up at Julia with tears in her eyes.

"It's impossible," she whispered.

There was nowhere to run, nowhere to hide. Maybe Julia was overdramatizing things, but she could barely breathe.

"Is it true?" Sally asked.

"What are you talking about?" Julia tried for casual, but she stumbled on the words.

"Oh, honey," she said softly. "He's Cameron's, isn't he?"

Julia felt her own eyes water as she slowly nodded.

"I thought so," Sally said, gazing back at Jake and touching his nose playfully. "That little dimple is better than a DNA test."

Julia had smiled, but her worry had increased. She could only hope Cameron took it this well when he finally learned the truth.

When Sally looked up again, she sniffled and said, "I'm in love with him already. Thank you so much." She wrapped Julia in a tight hug.

Completely distressed, Julia swore Sally to secrecy until she could break the news to Cameron herself.

"He doesn't know?" Sally had asked in shock. "Why on earth haven't you told him?"

Julia hastily explained that she'd tried, but Cameron had never called or returned her messages.

Sally rolled her eyes in exasperation. "Why am I not surprised? I'm sorry Julia, but my son can be stubborn."

Then Sally promised Julia that she wouldn't

say a word to Cameron. Her lips were pursed in determination as she called over the hotel manager and told him to put Julia and the baby in Cameron's suite. Julia had protested, but Sally managed to convince her that Cameron would be gone for the next two weeks.

"He'll never know what happened," Sally had said with an innocent smile. "Trust me."

Julia let herself into the suite and was surprised by the silence. There were no lights on, no sounds of activity anywhere. Back home, her house was never this quiet. Had Cameron taken the baby somewhere? Maybe Sally Duke had followed through on her promise to babysit and rushed up here to take the baby off to play.

Julia left her briefcase and purse on a dining room chair and considered pouring herself a glass of wine. The thought was irresistible but she would check on Jake first, then see about the wine.

It had been a long, intense day. She would have to talk with Cameron's mother eventually.

The fact that Sally had set them both up still baffled Julia. And she had to wonder what Sally would think when Julia told her that Cameron had discovered her in his shower.

"Maybe I won't go into quite so much detail," Julia muttered to herself. Removing her high heels, she walked down the hall to the baby's bedroom and still didn't hear anything. When she pushed the door open, the first thing she saw was the empty crib. She suffered a moment of consternation as she wondered where her baby could be. The room was dim with the lights off but the drapes were open, letting in the dusky twilight. Looking beyond the crib to the twin beds, she finally spotted Cameron laid out, with little Jake sprawled on his chest, sound asleep. Cameron's big hands were splayed protectively across the baby's back, holding him in place.

Julia's heart stuttered in her chest as she tried to swallow the emotional lump in her throat. Had she ever seen anything more beautiful than the sight before her?

Oh, she was in such big trouble.

She sighed, wondering if she could possibly be a bigger sap than she'd already been over Cameron Duke. There was no way she would fall for him again. Hadn't she learned her lesson about commitment-phobic men? Besides, she and Jake were doing just great on their own, thanks very much.

But now Cameron was back in the picture and he'd made a few things quite clear. First, despite his apparent affection for Jake, he didn't yet believe that the child was his son. Second, he'd like a repeat performance of the wild affair they'd had the last time they were together. But Julia had her child to consider now, and she was no longer interested in sex without love. Cameron wasn't about to open his heart to her, let alone fall in love and marry her.

And she was fine with that. She'd grown a lot stronger in the year and a half since Cameron had refused to answer her messages. She was happy. Her life was full. She neither wanted nor needed Cameron Duke in her life anymore.

No, the only thing she needed right now was someone who could convince her that everything she'd just told herself wasn't a big, fat lie.

# Four

Cameron heard a sigh and his eyes flew open. Julia stood a few feet away, staring down at him and Jake. She was still dressed in her serious business suit but she looked softer, almost more fragile now than she had that morning. He didn't budge from his position as he whispered, "He's asleep."

"I see that," she said quietly. "So were you."

"Nope," he countered. "Not asleep. Just resting my eyes."

"Ah." She smiled. "We should probably wake him up now or he won't sleep through the night."

Cameron frowned. "I never thought of that."

"That's okay, you didn't know," she said, walking to the edge of the bed.

Cameron patted and stroked Jake's back. "Hey, buddy, mom's home. Time for some grub."

The baby stretched and grunted. Cameron watched as he blinked, then stared into Cameron's eyes and began to whimper.

"Shh," Cameron said, as Jake's lips quivered. Concerned, Cameron shifted his gaze to Julia. "Why is he going to cry?"

"He's always a little crabby when he first wakes up from a nap," Julia said, reaching for the baby. "He's a bit disoriented and probably needs his diaper changed."

"Again?" Cameron frowned, feeling strangely bereft without the weight of the baby on his chest. "But the babysitter took care of that before she left."

"I'm sure she did," Julia said, smiling as she snuggled Jake against her shoulder. She slipped her feet into a pair of flat shoes she'd left by the bed. "But knowing Jake, I'd better check anyway."

"Okay," Cameron said, standing and stretching. "I'll watch what you do. Just so, you know, in case you're not around, I'll know what to do."

"Oh." She seemed taken aback, as though the thought had never occurred to her that he was capable or interested in taking care of the baby. "Okay. Good idea."

Sure enough, Jake needed a clean diaper in a big way. As Julia handled the task with an efficiency Cameron could only marvel at, she asked, "Did you speak with the nurse?"

It took him a moment to figure out what she was talking about. Then, for some reason, Cameron decided he wasn't quite ready to concede that Julia was right about Jake being his son. He'd let her squirm for a bit longer. "Oh, for the blood test? Not yet."

She sighed. "I don't know why you can't see it. Your mother knew Jake was your son within seconds. And before you jump to any conclusions, let me assure you that I didn't say one word to her. She just knew."

"My mother?" Cameron frowned. "She saw Jake?"

As she maneuvered Jake into some kind of stretchy blue pajama thing, Julia related what Sally had told her the day before.

"Okay, I'll admit my mother might have a scheme in mind," Cameron said, watching her. "That still doesn't mean Jake's my son. I mean, I can't imagine I'm the only guy you've ever…" Cameron couldn't continue with that thought. He didn't want to picture Julia with other men, not that it was any of his business what she did or who she did it with. He just didn't want to think about it. He coughed to cover his uneasiness. "Anyway, as I said before, we used protection. So you want to tell me how this could have happened?"

Julia raised her gaze to meet his. "Of course we used protection, but for goodness' sake, Cameron. Don't you remember how many times we did it that weekend? Something was bound to happen."

Yeah, he remembered. And even after all this time, Cameron's groin still stiffened at the memory of that red hot meeting of lips and tongues, hands, skin, bodies.

"Anyway," she said, after taking a deep breath, "you can blame your mother all you want, but we both know how *this* happened." Still blushing, Julia hoisted the baby up into her arms and rushed out of the bedroom. "I'll go warm a bottle and start his dinner."

Cameron followed, unwilling to end the conversation just yet. "Come to think of it, we wouldn't have met in the first place if my mother hadn't demanded that we carry your bakery stuff in our hotels."

She turned. "True. But that was almost two years ago now. Do you really think your mother was thinking at the time that we would…oh, never mind." Her chagrin was obvious as she hurried away from him and went to the kitchen. She placed the baby in his carrier on the bar and made sure he was secure, then walked over and opened the refrigerator door.

"That we would what?" Cameron asked provocatively. "That we would fall into bed the first night we met?" He came up close behind her and wrapped his arm around her waist to stop her in her tracks. "Or that we would spend seventy-two hours making love over and over again, until we passed out?"

He moved even closer. Her curvaceous bottom pushed against his erection and she moaned.

"Do you remember?" he asked.

"Yes," she whispered. "Thank God for room service or we might've starved."

He laughed, then groaned as she pressed into him. He kissed the skin beneath her ear. She stretched her neck to give him more access and he ran his tongue along her jaw line. "Do you remember drinking champagne in that big tub?"

"I remember," she whispered.

"God, you smell so good." He turned her around and kissed her cheek, her chin, then covered her trembling lips with his. Her mouth parted and he delved inside, exploring her moist heat with the sweep of his tongue. She sighed and he plunged again.

The doorbell rang and they both jumped, then stared at each other in disbelief.

"This is crazy," Julia muttered, and grabbed a bottle from the refrigerator shelf.

"Who the hell can that be?" Cameron groused and stalked to the door. He took a moment to compose himself before he opened the door.

"Hello, darling," his mother said.

"Yoo-hoo! Hi, Cameron," Beatrice said, waving behind her.

"We want to see the baby," Marjorie said. "We're not interrupting anything, are we?"

Cameron shook his head as the three women sashayed into the suite. They had been friends longer than Cameron had been alive. They still played cards together every Tuesday. Beatrice and Sally both volunteered at the hospital and Marjorie still worked as Duke Development's Human Resources manager.

"Hello, ladies," he said, and closed the door behind them.

"Are we too late?" Marjorie asked, glancing around the room.

Sally followed her gaze, then turned to Cameron. "We were hoping you'd let us babysit while you two kids ran out and grabbed some dinner."

Julia poked her head out from behind the kitchen bar. "Oh, no, that's not—"

"Sounds great," Cameron said immediately. "Give us five minutes and we'll be ready to go."

"They railroaded us," Julia grumbled as she sipped her chardonnay and nibbled on a carrot stick from the relish tray.

Cameron glanced around at the other tables in the elegant dining room of the Monarch Dunes. He was happy to see that there was a full house tonight, but the space still felt intimate. Stylized sconces along the sage-green walls cast dramatic shadows on the cathedral ceiling. Around the large room, screens and plants created a sense of privacy and exclusivity for the diners. The service was attentive yet discreet. And the food was excellent, naturally. The Duke brothers insisted on it.

"Do you really mind being out tonight?" he asked.

"Oh, no." She glanced around, admiring the room and the view. "Of course not. Everything is lovely."

"Good," he said, resting back in his chair. "Take a sip of your wine and relax."

She complied. "It's wonderful."

They were seated at a table along the glass wall overlooking the golf course and the cliffs and ocean beyond. It was a beautiful night, with a crescent moon and a million stars in the sky. The crystal glassware and silver flatware caught the candlelight and cast rainbow shards on the pristine white tablecloth.

He gazed at her through the glow. "I'm glad you like it."

Sighing, she said, "I just don't want Sally to think I expect her to babysit."

"Get used to it," Cameron said with a sardonic grin. "Now that she knows about Jake, you'll have a hard time keeping her away."

"I know," Julia said, smiling. "She's already threatened to pitch a tent on my front lawn so she can see him every day."

Cameron raised one eyebrow. "I'll talk to her if she gets pushy."

"Oh, goodness no," Julia said, and reached out to touch his hand in reassurance. "I think it's wonderful. I don't have any family so the thought of Jake having a grandmother to dote on him is like a dream come true."

Cameron held on to her hand when she tried to slip it away from his. "Speaking of family, I did what you suggested and looked up the Parrish Trust."

"So you know I'm not looking for a handout."

"No, I guess you're not," he said. "But when I was looking at the trust information, I saw that your parents died when you were young. I'm so sorry."

"Yes, they died in a plane crash. It was

devastating. I was ten years old and had no other family to live with."

"What happened to you?"

She smiled wistfully. "I had a nanny who'd been with me since I was born, so the judge allowed her to stay with me. My court-appointed guardians were two of my parents' lawyers and they moved into our house."

"You're kidding. You had lawyers for guardians?"

Julia grimaced. "Yes. And it was just as businesslike an arrangement as you can imagine. You know, I finally read my parents' will a few years ago and it made me feel like one of their properties. I know they loved me, so I blame it on the lawyers. It's just how they used to write these things. The bottom line was, neither of my parents had siblings so there were no relatives who could take me in."

"Be thankful you weren't put into the foster care system."

"Oh, I am," she said in a rush. "My nanny,

Rosemary, was great. She was like a mother to me."

"You were lucky to have her."

"Yes, I was." Julia fortified herself with another sip of wine. "But two years later, she died suddenly. Cancer. It was overwhelming. I cried for weeks."

"I'm sorry." He squeezed her hand lightly.

She nodded. "The trustees hired another nanny but she didn't do much. I was too old by then."

"You were only twelve."

"I always felt like a grown-up," she said, smiling as she broke a breadstick in half and munched on it. "My parents traveled quite a lot for their foundation so I was used to spending time alone. It was okay. I was a self-sufficient kid."

Cameron sipped his wine. "You were lonely."

"Oh, please," she said, waving the comment away. "Don't make me sound like some poor little rich girl."

"Why not?" Cameron's tone was so compassionate that Julia felt her eyes sting. Good grief, would she burst into tears merely because someone showed kindness to her?

"Because no one cares," she said. "Boo-hoo, all the money in the world but no one to love her. It's such a cliché."

"Clichés are true for a reason." Cameron put down his wineglass. "Some things are more important than money, Julia."

Did he mean *love* was more important? Julia wondered, but wasn't about to ask him out loud. Instead she said, "I agree, but it's easy for people with money to say it's not important. So rather than annoy my friends, I keep it simple and don't talk about myself."

"Except to me," Cameron said, and his lips twisted in a grin.

She frowned as though she'd just realized the same thing. "So it would seem."

The baby was asleep in his bed when they returned to the suite. Sally and her friends assured them they'd had the time of their lives and wanted to do it again. Then they said good-night.

"Would you like a nightcap?" Cameron asked, as he headed for the dining room liquor cabinet.

"I have a long day tomorrow," she said, tossing her sweater over the dining room chair. "But I wouldn't turn down a cup of hot chocolate."

"That's not quite what I had in mind, but okay." He shut the cabinet and followed her into the kitchen. "I'm not sure we have all the ingredients."

"We do." She pulled a slab of chocolate down from the cupboard and began to break it into chunks.

"Where did that come from?"

"I brought it with me," she said.

"You always travel with your own supply of chocolate?"

She looked at him as though he were a dimwit. "Of course."

"Oh, right, guess you never know when you'll be called on to make dessert."

"That's right." She placed the chunks in a small saucepan, added a touch of water and put it on the stove.

"That's it?" he said, his tone dubious.

She pointed to the pan, then the fire. "Chocolate. Hot. Equals hot chocolate."

"It seems like cheating."

She rested her fist on her hip. "You think I should carry cocoa beans and grind them to dust first?"

"Something like that."

She laughed. "This skips a step or two."

He gave her another skeptical look, then stared at the pan. "I'm not sure about this."

She stirred the mixture slowly. "Because you've always made it with cold milk and chocolate syrup."

"Well, yeah," he said, biting back a grin as he leaned against the bar. "Anything else is just un-American."

"Don't judge until you've tried it," she said mildly, adding some more drops of water as she continued to stir.

"It's starting to smell good."

"Here, you stir," she said, handing him the

spoon as she turned down the fire slightly. "I need to make whipped cream."

"I suppose you brought that with you, too."

"Always." She pulled a container from the fridge.

He couldn't hold back his smile. "I like the way you travel."

She reached into a drawer and pulled out her own hand mixer, poured cream into a bowl, threw in a heaping spoonful of sugar, and began to mix it up. Less than four minutes later, she had a bowl of thick, pillowy whipped cream. She poured the creamy chocolate into two small coffee cups, added a dollop of whipped cream on top, and handed one to Cameron.

"Sip the chocolate through the cream," she instructed. "That way, you get the hot with the cold, but you don't dilute either."

She stood inches away, watching him as he tried the concoction. He watched her, too, as he sipped the hot, creamy chocolate through the cool, soft whipped cream. It was possibly the most sweetly decadent thing he'd ever eaten.

"Well?" she said.

He stared at her and wondered what the chocolate and whipped cream might taste like when licked off her breasts.

"It's almost immoral, it's so good," he said, his voice husky.

Her cheeks began to turn pink again and he found he enjoyed making her blush. He also savored watching her realize the direction his thoughts were traveling.

She coughed to clear her throat. "So, you like it?"

"Like it?" He took another long sip and emptied the cup. "Yeah. I'd suggest you package it, but I'm afraid it might be banned in thirty or forty states."

"I'll take that as a compliment," she said demurely, and placed her cup on the counter. "Thank you."

"No, thank you. It was delicious." He put down his cup and reached for her. "I want to taste it on your tongue."

Before she could utter a word of protest, his mouth consumed hers.

The heat was instant and overwhelming. The sweetness of her mouth was incendiary. Pressing her against the kitchen wall, he kissed her again and his tongue swept inside, tangling with hers. Now he tasted the need in her. Now he sensed the surrender he'd craved from the first moment he'd seen her in his shower, her long legs wet and warm, her breasts firm and round. He wanted her with a fervent passion he hadn't felt in months, maybe years. Maybe since the last time he'd been with her.

He ravaged her mouth again and again, sweeping and plunging and reveling in her heated depths. She wrapped her arms around his neck and raised herself so that the apex of her thighs pressed against his burgeoning erection. He held her there with one hand while he shifted his other hand up to cover her breast. She moaned and he knew she wanted him as much as he wanted her.

His body shouted at him to take her here, now,

against this wall. Tear off her clothes and plunge into her over and over again until they both slid to the floor from sheer exhaustion. He couldn't remember feeling like this, couldn't remember ever needing a woman this much, as much as he needed another breath. Maybe more. She was his. Now.

Julia broke away to take a deep breath. "Oh, Cameron, I can't…"

"I know." He ran his mouth along her exposed jawline and down her neck, sucking and nibbling his way to her shoulders. He began to unbutton her blouse, pulling the fabric back to feast on her soft skin.

"Cameron, please," she murmured. "I…I'm sorry." She pushed away. "I can't do this. I can't…"

He groaned. "You can. You did. Watch. I'll show you."

She pressed her hand against his chest. "I know how it's done. I just…"

His brain clicked into gear and with great

reluctance, he shifted back a step. "You mean you're not ready to do this."

"Oh, I'm ready," she said with a contrite smile. "But I'm not stupid. I know how you feel, Cameron."

"I think it's pretty obvious how I feel," he said, carefully pressing himself closer.

It was her turn to groan. This felt too good, but she had to stay strong. "I mean, how you feel about *me.* You think I'm lying to you. You think I set you up and I'm trying to trap you into fatherhood."

"No, I don't."

"*Yes,* you do," she said calmly. "You have rules. I have Jake. We need to get through the blood test before we can even think about…well, I should go to bed."

*Crap,* he thought. The damn blood test. He really was a dolt.

"Julia, listen to me," he said with all the sincerity he felt in his heart. "I do believe you. I know Jake is my son. I haven't ordered the blood test because I know you're telling the truth."

Her shoulders sagged a little. "You're just saying that because we're this close to jumping into bed together."

"I'm not just saying it," he insisted, then gave her a sideways glance. "But is it working?"

She smiled softly. "I would love to be with you more than anything tonight. But it won't help matters at all. In fact, it'll just complicate everything."

He studied her for a moment and saw in her wide, expressive eyes a mix of storm clouds and uncertainty. And more than a remnant of passion. "I say we go with the complications."

Now Cameron could see a touch of sadness there in her eyes. It felt like a punch to the gut.

"I don't want to be with you simply because I happen to be the woman staying in your hotel suite."

"But you *are* the woman staying in my hotel suite."

"Exactly," she said. "Which makes me convenient, that's all."

"That's not what I meant." He swept his hands

through his hair in frustration. "I'm saying all the wrong damn things. Let's start over. I believe you, Julia. Jake is mine. I know you weren't lying. And I want you. I desire you. *You.* Not some woman sleeping in my suite."

She stared up at him, searching his face for answers.

"I want you, too," she said finally. "And I'm glad you believe me. But I know you have your rules. I know that once we leave here, you won't want me anymore. And I can't go through that. I won't. Not again."

Staring back at her, he saw the resolve. He also saw that if he continued his tender assault, he could melt away her reserve. But at what price? It wouldn't be what she wanted, what she needed right now. With great reluctance, he stepped back. "You're wrong, sweetheart. But I'm not going to convince you of that tonight, am I?"

She slowly shook her head. "I'm sorry."

"You and me, both." He couldn't help but lean over and kiss her full, ripe mouth once more. "Sweet dreams, Julia."

# Five

His freaking rules.

Talk about being hoisted by his own…whatever. Cameron punched his pillow, knowing once again that he wouldn't get much sleep tonight. It was just as well, because he needed to spend some quality time mentally kicking himself. And he really needed to rethink a few things. Like those rules of his. It's not that he would change them because, frankly, they worked. But he certainly wasn't going to talk about them anymore. Especially not to a woman who might've been lying in his bed this very minute, were it not for him and his big mouth.

Screw the rules, he wanted Julia.

How could he convince her that he believed her? He should've told her immediately that he knew Jake was his son. He'd known it almost from the first minute he'd seen the handsome little kid. But hell, that wasn't even Julia's point, was it? He smacked the mattress in disgust.

Whatever her point was, he still wanted her. Rules be damned. But if he tried to tell her that, she would think he was just saying it to get into her pants. And while that may be true…no, damn it, it wasn't.

He *liked* her. He liked her mind, and her sense of humor, and her integrity. Okay, he liked her pants, too, and everything inside them. Nothing wrong with that.

And besides, she was the mother of his child, so they'd be seeing each other at least once or twice a week for the foreseeable future. And since he'd be coming by to see Jake all the time anyway, why shouldn't they have a…a what? A relationship? An understanding? A regularly scheduled booty call?

Sounded good to him.

Oh, right, he thought. Even Cameron was smart enough to know she would kick his ass into next week if he suggested that scenario.

But she wouldn't keep him from seeing Jake. No way. Cameron would let her know in the morning they would need to work out a custody arrangement.

And now that he thought about it, he would have to make sure his house was baby-proofed. He made a mental note to call Housekeeping the next day and tell them to take care of it.

But just baby-proofing the house wouldn't make it a home for Jake. He would have to transform one of the bedrooms into a room for the little guy. A bed shaped like a race car. A computer. And toys. A football.

He would put up a fence around the pool immediately, but he would also teach Jake to swim as soon as possible. His son would be a champion swimmer.

He would build a super-deluxe swing set on the side of the house, with a slide and monkey bars to play on. And Jake would need a dog. A big one.

Cameron was just beginning to doze off when it occurred to him that the thought of Jake visiting once every few weeks didn't appeal at all. Maybe Julia and Jake should simply move into his sprawling home on the cliffs overlooking the bay. The place had six bedrooms. There was plenty of room for all of them and the kitchen was big enough for Julia's baking stuff.

Whoa. In a flash, Cameron threw off the covers and sat on the edge of the bed. "Am I insane?"

What was he thinking? He wasn't fit to be a father. And he had no business inviting Julia to move in with him. Hadn't he been through this before? Had he forgotten about Martina?

Years ago, long after the fiasco with his high school girlfriend Wendy, he'd left the marines and gone to work with his brothers to start up their development company. Through business acquaintances he met the very attractive Martina Moran. He thought he'd learned his lesson where love and women were concerned, but once he met Martina, his good sense flew out the window. She came on strong, and almost as a test of his own will he began dating her.

Their relationship flourished and he thought he might be falling for her. Anxious to prove he'd grown as a man and was no longer subject to his father's cruel legacy, he proposed, and Martina said yes. Cameron thought he might be able to finally relax and looked forward to many happy years of married life.

He had been young, stupid and oh, so wrong.

It turned out that Martina had been using Cameron to make another man jealous. Her scheme worked and that man, trust-fund baby Andrew Gray, had begged Martina to marry him. She walked out on Cameron as fast as her Jimmy Choo shoes could carry her.

Cameron had taken Martina's betrayal as a

message from the fates. His birthright could no longer be ignored and he had to force himself to accept that he was, indeed, a bad risk, a loser and irretrievably flawed. It was a hard lesson to learn, but it was for the best that he'd vowed never to give in to love again. It could end only in disaster.

He was older now, but was he any smarter? Could he actually make this work with Jake and Julia? Did he really have any choice in the matter? Jake was his son and Julia was Jake's mother. He was determined to make it work. Julia would have to understand that it was all for Jake. As long as they both had Jake's best interests in mind, everything would be fine.

He lay back down and as he drifted into sleep, a plan began to form in Cameron's mind.

It was an effort just to slide the key card into the door slot, Julia admitted the following eve-ning. She was exhausted. She hadn't slept well the night before and she'd just spent one of the most grueling conference days ever. She was looking forward to a glass of wine and a long soak in the tub after she got Jake settled for the night.

But as she stepped into the foyer of the suite, she was instantly assailed by the sounds of controlled madness. Music was playing and people were laughing and talking. Was Cameron having a party? Where was Jake?

Julia had just spent ten long hours working the conference. She was not in the mood for a party. Could she possibly get away with sneaking straight through to the hall and disappearing into the back bedroom?

But that would be a spineless act of cowardice. Julia considered the alternatives and decided she was okay with that.

Before she could make her move, though, a woman about her age walked into the living room and spied Julia lurking in the foyer.

"You must be Julia," she said with a smile. "Cameron's told us all about you."

And what was that supposed to mean? Julia wondered.

"Hello," Julia said, trying not to eye the other woman with too much suspicion. Not only was she drop-dead gorgeous and tall, with thick brown hair and perfect skin, but she looked really nice and friendly.

Was Cameron dating her? Not that she would blame him; the woman was lovely. But did he have to rub Julia's nose in it? Had he invited his friends over for a party? Julia was more convinced than ever that slinking off to the back bedroom was the way to go. She had no place here among Cameron's friends.

At that moment Sally Duke marched into the living room. "Trish, where is—" She stopped when she saw Julia and cried, "Oh, she's here!"

"Hi, Sally," Julia said, now thoroughly confused.

"Come in, sweetie. We've completely invaded your territory and you must be beat after that long day."

"That's okay," she said weakly.

"Come meet my boys and have a glass of wine. You've already met Adam's wife, Trish."

"Not exactly." Julia turned and smiled much more warmly and extended her hand to shake the other woman's. "Hi, Trish."

Trish ignored the handshake, instead pulling her close and giving her a hug. "I'm so glad to meet you. Jake is precious. We're all so lucky Cameron found you both."

"Thank you. I'm happy to meet you, too."

"I'm relatively new to the family, too," she said, linking her arm through Julia's. "Adam and I just got married a month ago."

"Oh, how wonderful. Congratulations."

"Thanks. We're really happy."

"Well, of course you are," Sally said with a wink. "I wouldn't have planned it any other way."

They both laughed, then Trish glanced at Julia. She must've been wearing a look of sheer bewilderment because Trish quickly said, "It's complicated."

Sally laughed again. "But you'll hear the whole story eventually. Come meet my sons."

Sally grabbed Julia's other arm and she and

Trish led Julia through the dining room and up to the kitchen bar.

The first thing Julia noticed was that the spacious kitchen area was literally dwarfed by three big, handsome men, obviously Cameron and his brothers, who chatted and laughed with Sally's girlfriends, Beatrice and Marjorie.

The next thing Julia noticed was that the largest of the brothers was holding her baby over his head as though Jake were a paper airplane about to be launched across the room. Jake screamed with laughter and excitement.

Julia, on the other hand, had to take some deep breaths in order to remain calm. This had to be Brandon who was holding Jake. Cameron had told her he used to be an NFL quarterback.

"I want to hold him," the third brother said. By process of elimination, this was Adam. Without waiting for an okay from Cameron, Adam reached over and grabbed Jake mid-flight.

Jake cooed with delight.

"Hi, Jake," Adam said, staring up at the baby. "Welcome to the family."

Brandon reached up and tickled Jake's stomach. "Hey there, kiddo. You're pretty happy to be here, aren't you?"

Jake giggled and his little legs bounced back and forth.

Brandon turned and thumped Cameron on the back. "He's awesome."

"Yeah, he is," Cameron said, taking the baby from Adam. Just for a moment, he held Jake close to his chest, and Julia could almost see his heart on his sleeve.

The moment passed and Cameron swung the baby up above his head so his brothers could get another good look at him. Jake continued to smile and coo at the men, thrilled to be flying in the air. Cameron brought the boy down to eye level and with a note of pride, said, "Notice how handsome he is? Looks just like his father."

"Aw, don't insult him like that," Brandon joked.

Adam laughed. "Yeah, this is a good-looking kid."

"Funny, very funny," Cameron said, and lifted his son up again.

"Dada!" Jake cried.

The room went silent. Julia watched the brothers exchange glances, then they all broke out in grins. Adam slapped Cameron's back. "Congratulations, Dad."

Cameron exhaled heavily. "Thanks, I guess."

"Yeah, congrats," Brandon said. "Can't wait to meet the little woman."

Trish coughed to get their attention. "The little woman?"

"Mama! Mama!" Jake cried. He waved his arms and kicked his legs as the three men slowly turned.

Julia had been marveling at the lovely camaraderie among the brothers and their willingness to bring Jake into the fold, but now she laughed at the abashed expressions on each of their faces. She reached out to pat Jake's cheek as he bounced in Cameron's arms. "Hi, punkin'. Are you having fun?"

The baby burbled and wriggled as Brandon shrugged. "Hey, I'm a big guy. Everyone looks little to me, not just women."

"Nice try, Ace," Adam drawled.

Ignoring him, Brandon thrust his hand toward Julia. "Hi, I'm Brandon, Cam's much smarter and more handsome brother."

Julia shook Brandon's large hand. He was as big as a bear and, like his brothers, one of the most handsome men she'd ever seen. He had shoulders as wide as the refrigerator and wavy, light brown hair an inch too long. He pushed his hair back, but several thick strands flopped onto his forehead, giving him an irresistible, bad boy look. Brandon looked powerful enough to snap a man in two with his bare hands, but he couldn't have been more gentle with Jake.

Adam stepped forward. "Hello, Julia. I'm Adam Duke."

She shook hands with the tallest and most serious of the three brothers. Adam was dark haired and sophisticated, with a strong jaw and piercing blue eyes that focused completely on her. Julia's first thought as she shook his hand was that Trish was a very lucky woman indeed.

"Adam's frightening the womenfolk again,"

Brandon said, and picked up his beer. "Listen, Julia, if you get scared and need a hug, I'm your man."

Julia laughed, and Trish rolled her eyes in amusement.

"Nobody's hugging her but me," Cameron muttered as he handed Julia a glass of crisp white wine. She smiled her thanks as his two brothers ribbed him.

Conversations overlapped as Cameron opened another bottle of wine. Everyone wanted to hold the baby, and Jake was perfectly happy to be passed around from one family member to the next. Not just the women, but Cameron's brothers also demanded quality time with their new nephew.

Julia took a sip of the wine and felt her muscles and nerves relax. A half hour had passed, she realized, and instead of feeling worn out, she felt energized. She'd never been around such a boisterous, fun group. If this was what family was all about, she would love to be a part of it always.

The doorbell rang and Sally ran out to see who it was.

"That'll be room service," Cameron said in a low voice behind her. "I hope you don't mind, but I invited everyone to stay for dinner."

"I don't mind a bit," she said, turning to smile at him. "Your family is wonderful. You're so lucky."

"I like to think so," he said, staring at her intently.

"I should help get things together," she said, feeling her cheeks burning. Cameron was the only man who could make her blush simply by looking at her.

As she gathered utensils, plates and napkins, she sized up the three Duke men. Cameron's brothers were both gorgeous, but Cameron eclipsed them both with his tall, leanly muscular body, clear green eyes and beautiful smile. And that adorable dimple in his cheek was like the cherry on top. No wonder she was always blushing when he was around.

As the room service crew worked swiftly to

set up dinner, Julia settled Jake in his high chair, placing Cheerios and soft baby carrots on his tray for him to munch on while she warmed his dinner.

Then, to everyone's delight, she whipped up a modified chocolate mousse by combining the remaining chocolate bars, whipping cream and sugar from last night and adding egg yolks and vanilla. Within ten minutes, dessert was chilling in the refrigerator and everyone sat down to eat.

All through dinner, they laughed and talked over each other, sharing lots of old family stories with Julia. One story would lead to another, and Julia couldn't remember a time when she'd laughed so much.

After the dishes were removed, Cameron made coffee, and Julia served her chocolate mousse to rave reviews. She had to laugh because it was one of the simplest things she could've made.

Back at the table after clearing the dessert dishes, Julia felt a little twinge in her heart at how readily the Duke family and friends had welcomed her and Jake into their lives. She watched as Cameron finished giving Jake his bottle and raised him to his shoulder. He rubbed the baby's back a few times and Jake favored him with a rousing belch. Everyone laughed and cheered.

Julia's breath caught as Cameron squeezed her thigh under the table. "You having a good time?"

She gazed at him. "The best ever."

These people, this moment, were exactly what Julia had dreamed about her entire life, she realized. It was the warm family circle she had always wanted to be a part of. Could it really be this easy for a dream to come true? Was she foolish to think she could honestly trust her heart to these people and this man?

Cameron had been watching her closely all evening. He didn't want to crow too loudly, but his plan was working to perfection, even better than he could've envisioned.

Leaning closer to Julia, he said, "Walk with me outside for a few minutes?"

"I should put the baby to bed first," she said.

"Oh, do you mind if we do it?" Trish asked, pushing away from the table. She stood and touched Adam's shoulder. "We should practice, you know."

Adam's eyes widened as he stared up at Trish.

"Excuse me," Brandon said, glancing back and forth at the two of them. "Do you two have an announcement to make?"

"I don't know," Adam said, his eyes narrowed on his wife. "Do we?"

She smiled innocently. "Of course not, but it never hurts to be prepared."

Adam's cheeks puffed out. Shaking his head, he stood and grabbed hold of Trish's hand. "Don't ever scare me like that again."

Everyone laughed, and Cameron handed the baby to Trish. "He's starting to fade into dreamland."

"He's so sweet," Trish whispered, then looked at Julia. "We'll be careful."

"He's pretty sturdy," she teased, tucking Jake's collar under his chin. "And he does love to get his diaper changed."

"Yeah," Cameron said with a laugh. "Good luck with that."

He led her out to the living room and opened the sliding glass door. Julia stepped out onto the terrace and he followed her. The evening breeze lifted her wavy blond hair and she pulled her lightweight jacket tighter around her waist. Cameron squelched the urge to wrap her in his arms and shield her from harm.

*It's just a little wind,* he thought, knowing she could take care of herself. But ever since he'd hatched his plan in the early hours of the morning, he'd been advancing, both mentally and physically, toward protective mode. He'd already called his housekeeping service to take care of the baby-proofing of his home. They'd also assured him they would have the swing set erected and ready to go within the week. Now he just needed to arrange for the baby's room to be fixed up. He was hoping Julia would be amenable to helping him with that job. They could go shopping together. Women loved to go shopping, right?

"What a beautiful view," she said, gripping the balcony rail as she stared north at the forest of towering redwood trees silhouetted against the night sky.

Cameron's gaze was focused on her. "Yes, it is."

Julia turned and saw that he was looking at her. It was too dark to see if she was blushing, but Cameron had no doubt her cheeks were pink. He wasn't sure why that made him smile. He just knew he hadn't met a woman capable of blushing in a long time.

"Are you having a good time tonight?" he asked, as he rested his hands next to hers on the railing.

"Yes," she said, and her eyes twinkled in the moonlight. "Your family is just wonderful. I'm so grateful that they've welcomed Jake."

"They've welcomed you, too, Julia."

"I know," she said, laughing softly. "They're so kind. I'm thrilled that Jake will grow up surrounded by a warm and loving family."

"Is it going to bother you to have us all clamoring to be with him?"

"Absolutely not," she said firmly. "That's the best thing in the world for him."

"I'm glad you said that, because it's something I've been thinking about all day."

"What do you mean?"

"I'm trying to figure out what's best for Jake."

She gazed up at him. "You are?"

"Yes," he said, smiling down at her. Damn, she was a beautiful woman. Sometimes that realization snuck up and knocked him upside the head. "I want Jake to be a part of my life, Julia. I want the very best for him."

She nodded warily. "I want that, too."

"Good," he said, pleased that his plan was working out so well. "Because I think you and I should get married."

# Six

"What?"

He knew he'd caught her off guard, so her shriek shouldn't have been such a big surprise to Cameron. But it still managed to ring in his ears. He grabbed hold of her hands in a romantic gesture he hoped she'd appreciate. "I want us to get married, Julia. You and Jake will move into my home. We'll be giving Jake a great life."

Julia's eyes turned dark. "Jake has a great life."

"It'll be even better if we're together," he said with all the patience he could muster.

"No," she said, shaking her head. "Absolutely not."

Not appreciating her tone, he stepped a foot back and folded his arms across his chest. "Are you going to keep me from seeing my son?"

Taken aback, she stared wide-eyed at him. "No, of course not. We can arrange some sort of visitation schedule. You can—"

"I don't want visitation," Cameron said. "I want him."

"That's not possible," she cried. "I'm his mother. He's been with me his entire life and I'm more than capable of raising him on my own. You can't take him from me."

"I don't want to take him from you," Cameron said quickly, annoyed that this conversation wasn't going the way he'd planned. Nothing seemed to go according to plan with Julia. "I'm asking you to marry me so we can raise him together."

She stared at him for a moment then asked, "What planet did you come from and what have you done with Cameron Duke?"

"That's not funny."

"You're right, it's not one bit funny. I don't know who you are. Where did you dream up this idea? There's no way I'm going to live with you."

"Why not?"

She spluttered in shock, but finally managed to speak in complete sentences. "Because you don't want me, Cameron. You never look back, remember? What happened to your rules? What changed overnight that you suddenly want me around?"

He swallowed hard and thought fast. "Look, people adjust, Julia. Rules are meant to change with the times." He was being perfectly reasonable, why couldn't she understand?

"Well, isn't that mature of you?" she said, a little too snidely for his taste. "But that still doesn't mean I'm going to move into your house to play nanny while you go about your business."

"Nanny?" He frowned. "Who said anything about you being a nanny?"

"Oh, come on, Cameron. I'm not a complete

idiot. You want Jake, so you need me there to take care of him."

"No, that's not true. I want you, too."

"Jake and I are perfectly happy in our own home. With *our* nanny. You can visit anytime."

"I don't want to visit, I want to live with my son and his mother. I want you to marry me. Why is that so hard to comprehend?"

"Because you're using me to get to Jake," she said, her voice quivering with emotion. "And I won't be used."

That's when it sank in. Julia was afraid. Damn it. Once more, he was being a dolt. She seemed to bring that quality out in him. Leaning back against the concrete balcony wall, Cameron pulled her close and ran his hands slowly along her spine, trying to soothe her. "I swear I'm not using you, sweetheart. I wouldn't do that. I'm just asking for a chance to live as a family. You, me and Jake."

She sighed, then looked up at him. "Cameron, you don't love me."

His eyes widened before he could stop the reaction. She wanted love? From him? He blew out a breath, knowing he could never give her that. But there were plenty of other things he could give her.

"Julia, I admire you," he said gently. "I respect you. I like you a helluva lot. I want to be with you. It's pretty obvious we're both hot for each other. That's a major plus, right? I think we could have a great life together. But I…I just don't do love. I'm sorry."

She tilted her head and studied him keenly. "Do you love Jake?"

He frowned. Did he love his son? Could he? He thought about it, remembering those moments when he and the little guy had stared into each other's souls. He already had a bone-deep connection to the boy. Was that love? Did it matter? Cameron didn't think so and Julia would have to deal with that.

"Jake is my son," he said. "I'll protect him with my life."

* * *

Julia nodded without speaking. She'd seen the look of awareness that had passed across Cameron's face when he'd considered whether he loved Jake or not. Julia knew that look. She'd seen it in her own face when she looked in the mirror while holding Jake. It was the look of parental love. Cameron might not be able to say the words, but she knew he felt them.

She didn't dare admit that she was tempted by his loveless proposal. What would that make her, besides desperate? Did she really want a family so badly that she would abandon the possibility of love forever?

A while later, she wandered through the rooms of the suite, visiting with the people she'd already begun to wishfully think of as her family. At the same time, she considered Cameron's words. He liked Julia. Respected her. They were hot for each other. But was all that enough to make them a family? On the other hand, there were probably plenty of other families that had started out with less.

A family was something she'd dreamed of for most of her life. She'd always imagined what fun it would be to have brothers and sisters to play with and talk to. Cameron's brothers and Trish would fulfill that desire. And with Sally, she would have a mom to share her deepest dreams and secrets with. They could go shopping and have lunch together.

"And we could braid each other's hair," she muttered, disgusted with herself. Good grief, was she so needy that she would marry Cameron just to have lunch with his mother?

With a sigh, she walked into the second bedroom just as Trish snapped the last snap on Jake's jammies.

"We did it," Trish said, gazing at Adam with justifiable pride.

"You were brilliant," he said. With one hand, he held Jake securely on the changing table while he reached for Trish with the other and planted a kiss on her mouth.

Julia sighed again. It was such a romantic move.

Trish noticed her then. "Oh, Julia, he was a perfect angel."

"And he looks relatively undamaged by the whole experience," Julia quipped. "For that, I thank you."

"Thank you so much for trusting us with him," Trish said.

Adam kissed her temple and she beamed at him. They were so clearly in love, it almost hurt to watch them.

Could Cameron ever love her that much? she wondered, then rapidly banished the foolish thought from her mind. Wishing for things that would never come true wasn't her style. Long ago, she'd trained herself not to wish for too much and to be happy with whatever she had, because things could always change for the worse in a heartbeat.

After Adam and Trish left the room, Julia laid Jake in his crib and rubbed his tummy until he settled.

"Sweet dreams, my darling," she whispered, and watched him drift off to sleep. He'd always been such a happy baby, and relatively easy to care for. Now Julia wondered if she was robbing her son of a closer relationship with his father by saying no to Cameron's proposition. Cameron had said he would protect Jake with his life. But was that enough on which to build a marriage? Could she be content, knowing that Jake would have a doting father who protected and cared for him?

As she switched off the light, Julia remembered the other point Cameron had made to sweeten the deal. They were hot for each other.

"So true," she murmured, and felt a jolt of desire in her lower stomach at the thought of the two of them in bed together. The image was so vivid, she had to stop for a moment, take a deep breath and let it out slowly, before she was able to walk into the living room. Her eyes instantly sought and found Cameron, who watched her with an intensity she'd never experienced from a man before.

Julia's laid-back facade turned to dust as Cameron's blazing awareness scorched her from across the room. Oh, yeah, they had heat. The question was how long could they make it last?

Cameron scrunched his pillow and wondered if he would ever sleep again. In keeping with his plan, after their guests had left, he'd led Julia to her bedroom door where he'd kissed her good-night and walked away.

"For the third damn night in a row," he said. Once again, he lay in bed wide awake, wondering what the hell was wrong with him. He was a marine, he'd led warriors into battle and faced the enemy, but walking away from Julia a few hours ago had been the hardest thing he'd ever done.

But it was for a good cause, he reasoned. His plan was working. Leave her wanting more. He'd give Julia another few days, but in the end, she would come to see that marriage was the best thing they could do for little Jake.

None of that seemed to matter to his libido,

though. He stared at the moonlight streaming in through the window and resigned himself to another sleepless night. All for the good of the plan.

It was impossible for Julia to avoid Cameron in the morning, not when he was sitting at the dining room table, eating toast as he fed Jake his breakfast of rice cereal and mashed bananas. She wondered how he'd picked up the baby's routine so well in less than three days. Was the babysitter giving him private lessons?

She also wondered if she would ever get a decent night's sleep again. It was bad enough that Cameron had dropped a bomb when he asked her to marry him. But then after that, when she'd gotten all hot and bothered and tempted by the way he watched her so intently, what did he do? He kissed her chastely and dumped her off at her bedroom door.

She hadn't slept a wink and it was all his fault.

"Jeez, kiddo," Cameron muttered, grabbing Jake's hand before he could smear bananas in his hair. "They go in your mouth, not in your hair."

Despite her somewhat surly mood, Julia bit back a smile. "Nice save."

He looked up and grinned and Julia's heart took a sharp dip. "Thanks. You off to the conference?"

"Yes," she said. "The babysitter should be here in five minutes."

"Okay, good," he said, as he took a cloth and wiped cereal off Jake's neck. Jake giggled and Cameron gave his nose a light tweak. Jake pounded his tray in delight and Cameron stroked his head affectionately. "Yeah, you're pretty tough, aren't you, pal?"

Julia's first baking demonstration was to begin in less than twenty minutes, but how could she leave when Cameron and Jake were having so much fun bonding, eating, playing? It was all so domestic. So normal and comfortable. So... desirable. She'd wanted this so badly, for so long, and now it was happening. How could she leave?

Not just today, but ever? How could she give this up?

The man and the baby laughed in unison and Julia stared, mesmerized. Dear God, was there anything more sexy than the sight of this strong man taking care of her baby?

The tears came from nowhere and Julia tried to sniffle them away. She had to go. Leave. Quickly, before her brain exploded from confusion, from distraction, from yearning. From love. Not to mention lust.

She took another deep breath and let it out, then leaned over and kissed Jake's cheek. "Bye-bye, sweetie. I love you."

Without thinking, she kissed Cameron as well, right on the mouth. Realization hit her and she tried to break off the kiss, but he grabbed her arm and kept her close, lengthening the contact until she gasped for air.

Breathless, she managed, "Um, bye."

"Bye-bye, sweetie," Cameron said, grinning brashly as she backed out of the room and rushed out of the suite.

* * *

The meeting with the new investors had gone smoothly, Cameron thought, as he slipped their business cards inside the pocket of his suit jacket. Now he had an hour to kill before he met with his managers for their weekly lunch. Strolling down the wide hall to the conference center, he found the demonstration room he'd been looking for and walked inside.

"Can you taste the difference?" Julia was saying as she wandered up the aisle, holding a large bowl and handing out samples to the attendees on small plastic spoons.

"It's so bright, it practically glows," she said cheerfully. "I love that. And see how sticky it is? That's from the egg whites. This type of frosting takes longer to make, but look at the stiff peaks. It's gorgeous, isn't it? Worth the extra effort, don't you agree?" Julia popped a sample into her mouth. "Mmm, and so sweet, it melts on your tongue."

Cameron was hard in an instant. It didn't seem to matter that the room was filled with people, or that she was dressed conservatively in sensible heels, slim navy pants and a pale blue shirt with a cook's apron tied securely around her waist. He wanted her now. He could imagine her in just the apron and heels and his hardness intensified.

Gritting his teeth, he wondered how an innocuous, twenty-second description of cake frosting could make him want to pick her up and toss her onto the nearest flat surface where he could plunge into her hot, moist core?

Maybe it was her vocabulary. Sticky, stiff peaks? Melts on your tongue? Damn, just what was she teaching these people?

At that moment, Julia saw him and stopped in her tracks. His gaze narrowed in on her and he wondered if she could see what she was doing to him.

Her eyes flashed with awareness and she had to cough to clear her throat. "We'll take a ten-minute break now, and when you come back, I'll reveal the secret ingredient for making the ultimate buttercream frosting."

Cameron ignored the stream of attendees

drifting past him and stared directly at Julia until the room had cleared and she approached.

"What a nice surprise," she said with a smile. She still held the bowl of frosting and scooped out a small spoonful. "Want a taste?"

"Yeah," he growled. He grabbed the bowl and spoon and put them on the nearest desk. Then he clutched her upper arms, pulled her close and kissed her. He could taste the sweetness on her lips, her tongue, and wanted more. Wanted all of her. Here and now.

She reached up and wrapped her arms around his neck and he knew she could feel his length pressing against her.

"Where can we go?" he demanded. "Right now. Where can we be alone?" He didn't know why he was asking her. Hell, he owned the place, he ought to be able to come up with something. But with her clinging to him, his mind was a sieve. He couldn't think, couldn't focus, couldn't do anything but take as much of her sweet heat as she could offer.

"Cameron," she whispered, panting for air. "My students will be back in a minute."

"I want you now," he said, as if she couldn't tell from the rock-hard pressure against her. His mouth covered hers in a move of possession so demanding that she could only comply, opening to allow him entry so deep that he wondered vaguely where he left off and she began.

"Cameron, I...I want you, too," she said on a gasp of air. "But we'll have to wait."

"I can't wait much longer," he muttered, then took her mouth again, sweeping inside to savor more of her moist warmth.

"Tonight," she promised when they broke off the kiss.

"Tonight," he echoed, just as the doors swung open and her students filtered back into the room.

"And we'll talk," she added.

"Yeah, we'll talk."

# Seven

Julia stepped inside the suite and glanced around the quiet, empty living room. Were Cameron and Jake taking a nap again?

A sudden, distant whoop of laughter made her smile, and she followed the shrieks and giggles all the way back to the bathroom attached to the second bedroom. Taking one cautious look inside the room, she burst into laughter herself.

Jake sat, surrounded by floating toys and securely tucked into his sturdy bath ring seat. The seat was suctioned to the bathtub's surface so he couldn't go anywhere, but he could splash up a storm. And that always made him happy.

Cameron, on the other hand, was drenched. "Partner," he said, as he soaped up a washcloth and swiped it across Jake's shoulders and back. "We're going to have a long talk about water conservation one of these days."

Julia smiled. She'd spent the morning going over all the pros and cons of a marriage to Cameron Duke, but when he'd walked in on her frosting workshop earlier, she forgot everything she'd been thinking. The look in his eyes as he'd stared at her told her everything she needed to know. Maybe he didn't love her yet, maybe he would never use the *L*-word with her, but in that moment, in his eyes, she had seen something so intense, so real, so elemental. Part of her wanted to take that leap of faith, to be part of his life, to be a family with him and wanted to experience his passion every day for as long as it lasted. But another part of her was holding back, worrying and wondering if a loveless marriage to Cameron was perhaps the worst thing she could commit to, for both of them.

Cameron looked up at her then, his face dripping water. "Do you want to take over here?"

"No, you're doing great," she said, and made her escape.

An hour and a half later, the dinner dishes were in the dishwasher and a sleepy Jake was tucked into bed.

Cameron tugged Julia's hand and they tiptoed out of the baby's room. He led her into the living room where he'd left their half-full wineglasses and a small plate of her homemade cookies. "Let's sit here and talk."

"Okay," she said, visibly nervous. He wasn't sure why. She held all the cards in this transaction, didn't she know that?

When the idea had first occurred to him to have Julia and Jake move in, the thought of asking her to marry him was the furthest thing from his mind. After all, from the time he was eight years old, he had vowed never to get married, ever. Of course, he'd also vowed never to have children. So much for the vows of an eight-year-old boy. Now, not only did he have a kid, but he fully intended to move that kid into his home and marry his mother—if that's what it took to get them there.

He hoped he'd made the case last night, that their marriage would be built on respect and a mutual desire to raise Jake in a two-parent home. And lots of hot sex, of course. That was a key point of the negotiations.

And that was a hell of a lot more than most people started with.

"Cameron, I've—"

"Sweetheart, just—"

She laughed self-consciously, and Cameron said, "Go ahead. Tell me what you were going to say."

"Okay," she said with a nod as she brushed her hair away from her face.

"Here, let me do that," Cameron murmured, and ran his fingers through her thick, luxurious strands, lifting and pushing them back. He used the movement to come closer and breathe in her feminine scent.

"That feels good," she whispered.

"God, you're beautiful," he said, clutching her hair lightly in his hands as he stared into her vivid blue eyes. A few errant wisps of hair got loose and he smoothed them back behind her ears. "Your hair is every color of the rainbow."

"I know," she said shyly. "It's so odd."

"It's lovely." He bent to kiss her neck. "And it always smells great."

"Thank you," she said. Her eyelids fluttered closed and she moaned as he kissed her once more. "You're distracting me, you know."

"I know," he said, as he nuzzled her neck. "Give me a minute."

She touched his cheek. "Cameron, I'll never say what I need to say if I don't do it right now."

"All right," he said in resignation, and sat back against the cushions. "Go ahead."

She took a deep breath, looked him directly

in the eyes and said, "Okay. It's just that I…I've decided that, yes, I'll marry you."

He'd always known—hoped—he'd be able to talk her into it, but he hadn't realized until that moment how immensely important it was that she agree. He felt himself loosen up as his muscles relaxed and his chest lightened, making him realize he'd been tense enough to crack in half.

"Did you just say you'll marry me?" he said, checking to make sure he'd heard her correctly.

"Yes," she said, smiling tentatively. "Yes, Cameron. I'll marry you."

"Good. That's settled." He swooped her off the couch and onto his lap, then cut off her next sentence by kissing her deeply. His hands traced the length of her spine as his mouth claimed her as his own. His body absorbed the waves of shivers radiating off her as she met his fervor wholeheartedly, opening for him in a charged meeting of lips and tongues and anticipation.

He savored the taste of her and wanted to feel her skin against his. Now.

Julia must've had the same thought because she wriggled off his lap and turned to straddle him. "Touch me," she demanded.

"Great minds think alike," he murmured, as he slid his hands under her sweater. Lifting it up and off her in one movement, he inhaled sharply at the sight before him. She was braless. Her breasts were exposed and they were perfect. Fuller than he remembered, ripe and round, her dusky pink nipples erect as if waiting for his touch.

With both hands, he cupped her breasts, using his thumbs to tease her nipples until she moaned and pressed her hands over his. He gave in to temptation and moved to take first one breast, then the other into his mouth, licking, sucking and nibbling as she whispered words of urgent need.

Delicious, was all he could think. His senses were spinning out of control. Her skin was silken. She smelled like a field of delicate flowers and tasted like the sweetest sin.

Julia's hands moved to his head and clutched him to her breasts, urging him to indulge more.

Any thoughts of taking things slowly disappeared as he drank her in, moving back to her succulent mouth where she met him hungrily, opening for him to sweep in and take.

Scorching a path down her neck, he kissed his way across her shoulders and back to her breasts, which demanded more attention from him. She moaned as her hips moved back and forth, pressing against him insistently. His erection strained for release. He was dangerously close to losing it and she and her sexy body weren't helping matters.

"You're killing me," he growled. "Wrap your arms around my neck." Gripping her bottom with both hands, he levered himself off the couch and stormed down the hall to the master bedroom where he laid her on the bed.

She leaned up on her elbows and watched as he rapidly stripped off his clothing. Her eyebrows rose as his erection was unfurled. He could see the hunger in her eyes and it empowered him. He prowled closer, naked and rigid, until he stood between her legs. Bending over her, he unzipped her pants and pulled them off, leaving her in nothing but an incredibly hot, black lace thong.

"Is it my birthday?" he wondered aloud.

"Did you make a wish?" she asked, her eyes twinkling with promise.

"Yeah. It just came true."

She licked her lips in an unconscious move that almost undid him. Then she blinked in surprise as he knelt at the end of the bed and shifted her legs onto his shoulders.

"I have to taste you," he muttered, and kissed her most delectable spot. When he thrust his tongue into her, she arched off the bed with a feral cry.

"You're mine now," he murmured, and proceeded to brand her, licking and plunging over and over until she was writhing on the bed. He used one finger to enter her moist core and she groaned with pleasure.

"Now, Cameron," she cried. "I need you inside me now."

He lowered her legs carefully, then stood and walked across the room, leaving her moaning in protest until she noticed him putting on a condom. Then he was back. He knelt on the bed and stroked her again with his fingers to assure himself she was truly hot, moist and ready for him.

"Please, now," she whispered, pulling him closer.

"Yes, now," he said and entered her swiftly and completely. She gasped and he planted his mouth on hers and kissed her fully, swallowing her cries, sweeping within, his tongue matching his own surging thrusts as he buried himself within her.

She drove him to the edge, but his innate self-control pushed back from the brink. Pumping harder, faster, he moved deeply into her, so deep that he might've lost himself in her. It didn't matter. Pulling his head back, he watched the storm gather in her eyes as he stroked again, craving more, demanding all. When at last he saw her head whipping back and forth in surrender and heard her cry out his name, he buried his face in her neck and kissed her skin. Gathering the last of his strength, he thrust again, then again, and finally gave himself up to the abyss and tumbled, free-falling, into her arms.

They were married three days later on the cliffs of the Monarch Dunes resort, overlooking the ocean. The day was sunny and bright, the ocean was a calm, deep blue, and the grass was sparkling green after an overnight light spring rain.

All in all, it was impossibly romantic, or it would've been, if not for the fact that the groom didn't love the bride. And the lawyers on both sides who'd insisted on drawing up a prenuptial agreement. Cameron and she had signed the final documents that morning.

But Julia refused to dwell on the gnawing details as she listened to her new husband declare, "I do." A minute later, he wrapped her in his arms and kissed her senseless in front of the small crowd of well wishers, and all seemed right with the world.

She'd found a beautiful white dress to be married in. It wasn't exactly the bridal gown of her dreams and maybe the white was a bit of a stretch but it was a lovely off-the-shoulder summer frock that she could wear again. Cameron looked handsome and strong and sexy in his tuxedo. Sally and Trish had found an adorable matching tuxedo for little Jake to wear.

"I'd like to make a toast," Adam said, and everyone raised their glasses as he proceeded to give a stirring speech.

"Cheers," the guests cried, and Cameron and Julia took sips of the expensive champagne. The diamond on her finger twinkled and she smiled. The day after she'd told Cameron she would marry him, he had presented her with the most beautiful ring she'd ever seen. Then he'd made love with her so tenderly, so sweetly, she'd been brought to tears. Yes, she knew Cameron didn't love her, but she couldn't fault him for putting on a really good act.

Julia had been consumed by both the catering conference and the sudden wedding plans, so Sally had taken on the task of inviting friends to the wedding. Many of Julia's friends were there today, and for that alone, she fell in love with her new mother-in-law all over again.

Cameron's two brothers were sharing the best man honors. Sally had held Jake quietly through the ceremony and the toast, but now the boy cried for Cameron to hold him.

"Come here, cowboy," Cameron said, and hoisted Jake into his arms, putting an immediate stop to the whimpering. Holding Jake securely in one arm, Cameron put his other arm around Julia, then leaned in to kiss her. "Thank you. We'll be happy, you'll see."

"I know," she said, smiling. Then she was whisked away for a hug and a kiss on the lips from Brandon.

"Welcome to the family, gorgeous," he said.

She smiled up at her handsome new brother-in-law. "Thank you, Brandon."

"I'd like to welcome you, as well," Adam said,

then hauled her into his arms and kissed her soundly.

Dizzy, she almost stumbled but caught herself. "Whew. Okay. Anyone for cake?"

Cameron scowled at his brothers, but Sally laughed as she linked arms with Julia. "They're a formidable trio, aren't they?"

"I'll say," Julia said, still breathless.

"This is a delightful party," Sally said, giving her a quick hug before she left to join her girl-friends at the champagne bar.

Julia watched as other guests wandered over to the nearby tables where all sorts of hearty hors d'oeuvres shared space with numerous bite-sized desserts. Many of them were made following her own recipes so she knew they were delicious. She wished she'd had more time to prepare for the wedding, but things had turned out pretty well, under the circumstances.

Most importantly, she and Jake were now part of a family, and that made all the last-minute preparations worth it.

Her old friend Karolyn Swenson walked over and gathered her close for a hug.

"I'm so glad you could make it," Julia said. They'd known each other since grade school and Karolyn was her manager at the bakery.

"How could I miss it?" Karolyn said, gripping Julia's hands in hers. "I still can't believe you're married. You actually went and did it."

"I did it," Julia said, and met her friend's gaze. "Be happy for me?"

"Of course, I'm happy for you," she said, then whispered, "He's gorgeous. I assume he's your baby's daddy. Jake looks just like him."

Julia gave a start of surprise. "Yes, he's the one. And he'll be a great dad. We're going to be a happy family."

"Then that's all that matters, isn't it?" Karolyn hugged her again, and Julia had the feeling her friend was trying to reassure her that she'd done the right thing.

As Karolyn walked away to find a glass of champagne, Julia's resolve slipped. Was having a family all that mattered? Julia had thought so when she told Cameron she'd marry him, and again when she said "I do" a while ago. But honestly, how would she know? She hadn't had a real family in almost twenty years. But it's what she'd always wanted, so she would have to take it on faith that she was doing the right thing. Faith, and Cameron's vow that the three of them would have a wonderful life together. As vows went, that was a good one.

"I brought you a fresh glass of champagne," Sally said.

Julia turned and smiled her thanks and the older woman entwined her arm in Julia's.

Sally sighed. "When I see the way Cameron looks at you, it warms my heart."

Julia counted to five to ease the sudden tension she felt. "I know we'll be really happy together."

"Of course you will be." Sally patted her arm. "Now look, you and I were friends long before we became family, right?"

"That's right," Julia said with a tentative smile.

"So I want you to tell me the truth. You do love Cameron, don't you?"

Julia blinked. "Love him? Why, of course I…"

Sally studied her for a moment. "Was that a yes?"

"Oh, God," she said lamely. It was impossible to lie. The fact was, she and Cameron had talked about his inability to love her, but as for whether Julia loved him or not…

What she knew for sure was that she wanted to be part of his family more than anything. She respected and cared for him a lot. She wouldn't have agreed to marry him if she didn't.

Her shoulders sagged. "I don't know."

"You don't know?" Sally asked. "Interesting. It didn't come up in conversation before you took the plunge?"

Julia bit her lip. "Well, yes, it did. But not in the way you think."

"I suppose I appreciate your honesty," Sally said. "But I'm going to go out on a limb and say that I won't be surprised if someday soon, you and Cameron both realize that what you're feeling for each other is love."

Julia grabbed Sally's hand and squeezed. "I

hope you're right. But for now, please know that I'm happy. Really, really happy."

"I'm happy, too, sweetheart." Sally blinked back tears, then smiled and surveyed the crowd. "I'll be honest. Once my sons were grown, I worried that they would have a hard time finding women who would love them for themselves and not for their money or position."

"I imagine you've suffered through some scary moments over that issue."

"You'd better believe it." She winked at Julia. "But I don't have to worry about that with you, do I?"

Julia laughed. "No, I don't think anyone can accuse me of marrying your son for his money."

"What's so funny?" Cameron said, coming up behind her. He wrapped his arm around her waist and pulled her close to his side.

"Sally was just saying that nobody can accuse me of marrying you for your money."

He chuckled, then thought about it for a moment. "I guess nobody can accuse me of that, either."

"So it's a win-win," she said and smiled at him.

"Absolutely," he murmured, and smiled back. Then he tightened his hold on her, pulling her even closer and resting his forehead against hers.

Sally looked on with interest, then said something about getting more champagne and walked away, leaving the newlyweds alone for a moment.

He stared into her eyes. "Have I told you lately how beautiful you are?"

She sighed. He was so handsome, and he'd been so good to her and Jake. It wouldn't take much more for her to fall in love with him.

She stopped, stunned. What was wrong with her? Hadn't she just confessed to Sally that she hadn't married for love? She needed to get a grip. He was handsome and a nice guy, so all she was feeling was lust, not love. She glanced around as she cleared her throat. "It looks like everyone's having a good time."

"Thanks to you," he said. As his brothers came over to talk to him, Cameron absently took hold of Julia's hand and kissed her knuckles.

She sighed again. It had just been a momentary

lapse, she assured herself. It wouldn't happen again. She could blame it on the wedding itself. Weddings were romantic, that was a given. Everyone here, including his mother, had automatically assumed they were in love. And why wouldn't they? She and Cameron had just repeated vows to love and honor each other. They were married now. Both of them wore shiny new wedding rings. They'd put on quite a show.

But that's all this was. A show. A sham, really. Cameron was not in love with her, never would be. And if she thought about it, she couldn't really be in love with a man who didn't love her, could she? No. And if she found herself wishing, just once in a while, that he really did love her, then she was a bigger fool than anyone.

It was time for her to face the fact that all she had with Cameron Duke was a marriage of convenience. With benefits, of course. Rather nice benefits, to be sure, but those were a far cry from love everlasting. And the sooner she accepted that reality, the better off she would be.

# Eight

That evening, Sally took the baby and all his baby necessities to her room for Jake's first sleepover. For Sally, it was an adventure. For Julia, it was an excuse to worry.

Cameron ordered champagne to go with some of the hors d'oeuvres they'd brought back from the wedding ceremony. Julia changed out of her white dress and into something cozier while Cameron poured the champagne.

As she walked into the living room, she stopped abruptly. "Did your mother take the wet wipes with her?"

"I don't—"

"I'd better check." She turned and ran back to the bedroom, then returned after a few seconds. "I guess she got them."

"Julia, relax," Cameron urged, and handed her a fresh glass of champagne.

"You're right, I'm being silly." She took a sip and started to sit down on the couch, then jumped up. "Oh, no. I forgot to give her the brush for washing out the bottles."

"Sweetheart, my mother is not going to wash baby bottles."

"Oh, God, of course not. What was I thinking?" She took another sip of the champagne, then sighed. "I guess I just miss him."

Feeling relaxed, Cameron leaned his elbow on the mantel. "Hey, at least you've had him around for the past nine months. How do you think I feel? I just…"

He cut himself off as he saw Julia's eyes narrow in on him like a heat-seeking missile. He wondered if it was possible to snatch the words back, but it was too late. She turned on him like a rabid dog. "So you still blame me for keeping him from you?"

"No, I don't," he insisted with a firm shake of his head.

She walked right over and smacked his arm. "All it would've taken was one lousy phone call, but you were too damn proud to give an inch."

"You're right, sweetheart. But at the time, it seemed like you were a little obsessed."

She stopped in her tracks and turned on him. "Obsessed? I was not obsessed. I was—" she flailed her arms, trying to find the right word "—I was driven."

He realized they'd never truly discussed all her emails or his blatant disregard of them. Tonight didn't seem like the most opportune time to delve into it, but the subject wasn't going to go away. "Look, you sent me four emails in one day, Julia. I'd call that a little obsessive."

She folded her arms tightly across her chest. "So you actually saw my emails."

"Yes, I saw them," he said reasonably. "I opened the first one where you demanded that

I call you. And I almost picked up the phone, but then I noticed you'd sent three more in rapid succession and I figured you were a little, you know."

"Obsessed," she said pointedly, and continued her pacing.

He shrugged. "I guess. But that's all in the past. Let's forget about it and enjoy the evening."

But she wasn't ready to let it go. He was troubled that she was no longer fuming but instead looked a bit forlorn. "I was pregnant and alone, Cameron. Nobody would've blamed me for being a little obsessed."

"I don't blame you," he said. "I'm just explaining how I felt at the time. In hindsight, I wish I'd called you, but back then, I was being cautious."

"Oh, because so many women are obsessed over you?"

He wasn't about to explain to his lovely new wife that there actually had been a few dangerously obsessed women over the years. Right now, Julia was venturing into perilous territory and Cameron didn't see a safe way out.

"Look Julia, you're upset and—"

"You're darned right I'm upset."

"Then let's sit down and talk about—"

"Never mind, Cameron," she said, pacing away from him, then whirling around. "I'm sorry, but I can't do this right now. I need some time to think. I— I'm sorry." She turned and ran down the hall to the second bedroom where she went inside and closed the door.

"That did not go as planned," he muttered, staring down the hall, almost not believing what had just happened. He'd screwed things up royally. He wasn't sure how, he just knew this was his fault.

The fact was, they were married now. They shouldn't be fighting, they should be having sex. Rubbing his forehead in frustration, he walked to the wet bar and poured himself a healthy shot of Scotch. Holding the glass up, he toasted himself. "You're a knucklehead." The whiskey burned all the way down his throat. And so did the realization that he'd hurt her.

But she'd caught him off guard. He was so used to Julia being reasonable and smart and funny, he hadn't recognized the signs. She'd worked night and day to put together the wedding. And she'd been worried about the baby. He didn't realize how worried, so he hadn't helped matters one bit.

Fortified by several more generous slugs of Scotch, he flopped down on the living room couch, thinking he'd watch the football game. But he dozed off before he ever had a chance to switch on the television.

Something was pounding against his head. Had he really had that much to drink last night?

"Dada!"

Cameron opened one groggy eye and saw a blurry-looking Jake, up close, smacking his little hand against Cameron's forehead.

"Hey, buddy," Cameron whispered, grabbing his hand. "Let's use our indoor voice, okay?"

"Dada," Jake cried in excitement, then bobbled and plopped back on his well-padded butt.

Cameron's vision began to clear and he could now see Julia standing a few feet away, her arms folded across her chest, shaking her head at him.

"Don't yell," Cameron said in surrender. "I know I'm a slug and deserve your wrath, but I want you to be happy and I want us to be together. I apologize for everything. Can we start this whole thing over?"

She smiled, enjoying the moment. "I'd like that."

That night, Cameron was determined to seduce his wife. This time, he did everything right. The baby was off to spend the night with Sally again, he'd stocked up on more champagne and ordered a small platter of appetizers. And there was Julia.

Sitting on the couch, he framed her face with his hands and gazed into her eyes. "Forgive me, Julia."

"Of course," she said simply.

"I don't really want to get too far into it," he

said, "but I've lived with anger in my life. Let's make a pact never to go to bed angry again."

She searched his face and must've found whatever it was she was looking for, because she nodded. "It's a deal."

"Good." He kissed her. Then he reached inside his pocket. "I have something for you. A token of my feelings for you, as well as my gratitude, and…well. Here."

He pulled out a slim blue box and handed her the gift.

"No." She stared at the box, then looked at him, her forehead creased with concern. "I didn't get you anything."

He chuckled. "Honey, I already got the best end of the deal. I got you and Jake."

She carefully unwrapped the baby-blue jeweler's box and opened the lid. Inside was an exquisite diamond necklace. In shock, she whispered, "Oh, Cameron, it's gorgeous. But…why?"

"Because I wanted to give you a little something to remember this evening. Now let me put it on you."

"It's hardly 'a little something,'" she murmured, but held her hair up as he slipped the necklace around her neck and fastened it.

He kissed the back of her neck, then she turned to show him how it looked. "It's perfect. Just like you."

She smiled as she ran her fingers hesitantly over the necklace. "You shouldn't have done it, but thank you."

He poured champagne, then they made slow, easy love on the couch. Afterward, they moved to the bedroom and started all over again.

Much later, they were both too wide awake to sleep, so they talked for another hour. Cameron asked her questions about her pregnancy and Jake's birth. She told him about the baby's milestones. He wondered about their nanny and she told him all about the older woman who took such good care of Jake. They talked about her bakery and her schedule these days.

He asked her why she specialized in cupcakes at her bakery. She shrugged, told him that people liked cupcakes, then changed the subject, asking him how it was to grow up with two brothers. He regaled her with Sally Duke stories. Cameron found himself laughing more than he ever thought he could.

The laughter turned to kisses and they ended up making love again.

The next morning, they shared a quiet breakfast on the terrace, wearing matching robes. He was pleased that she still wore the diamond necklace.

"Do you want more coffee?" he asked, lifting the carafe.

"Yes, please." She glanced around, a puzzled frown on her face. "Is that water running?"

He listened, then grinned. "It's the waterfall."

"You have a waterfall?" Standing, she walked to the balcony railing and looked out at the resort grounds. "Is it by the beach?"

"Not exactly." He joined her at the railing and pointed out a large, thick copse of trees and shrubbery next to a rocky mound halfway across the expanse. "It's a pool. Very private. We rent it out for parties occasionally, but we don't advertise it. It's part of an underground spring, so the water is naturally warm. I had a grotto built around the pool, with a waterfall. It's pretty nice."

She sighed. "It sounds wonderful."

"It's secluded and romantic." He wrapped his arms around her. "Maybe we'll check it out before we leave."

"I have only two days left of my conference, so we'll have to…oh, my God."

"What is it?"

Her eyes showed a spark of fear. "What day is this?"

"Tuesday."

"Cupcakes," she cried. "I have to bake cupcakes." She slid the terrace door open, then stopped and shook her finger at him. "You distracted me."

"I hope to God I distracted you," he muttered, following her into the suite.

"Oh, you know what I mean." She circled the kitchen, opening cupboards and slamming drawers. "The demonstration is today at two o'clock. I have to start baking now."

"Why don't I just send my assistant to the store to buy a few dozen cupcakes?"

She stared at him, her mouth agape in horror. She waved him off as she raced down the hall. "You don't get it."

"Babe, relax," he said, strolling after her. "I can help."

She stopped abruptly. "Very funny, Cameron."

"Hey, I'm a good cook," he insisted, scowling as he trailed her into the master bathroom. "Ask anyone. I'll pit my chili recipe against anyone's, any day of the week."

"Your *chili* recipe?" she said. "Cute."

"Okay, those are fighting words." His eyes narrowed as she ignored him, whipped off her bathrobe and stepped into the steaming rush of water.

"So maybe we'll fight later," he muttered, then threw off his robe and followed her into the warm shower.

* * *

The kitchen bar became an assembly line with all three of Julia's professional-strength mixers arranged side by side.

On another counter, she'd lined up all the ingredients she would need, as well as the bowls, spoons, measuring cups and spatulas she would use to blend everything together.

Cameron had called Sally to ask if she could keep the baby for a few more hours while he and Julia baked cupcakes. Sally and her girlfriends were thrilled. Jake could sit in his bouncer while the women played canasta by the pool.

"Okay, let's get this show on the road," Cameron said, all business as he tied a cook's apron around his waist. "How much flour do you need?"

"Baking is slightly different than cooking," Julia said warily. "I won't be offended if you just want to sit at the bar and offer moral support."

"You're kidding, right?

She sighed. "Okay. We'll need three cups of flour in each of those three large glass bowls."

"Fine." He reached for one of the glass measuring cups and the bag of flour.

"Oh, use this plastic cup, not the glass one."

"What's the difference?"

She held up the two different measuring cups. "One's for liquids and one's for solids. You can fill this one to the top and level it off." She demonstrated how to level it off using the thin, straight handle of the spatula.

Cameron considered that, then nodded.

Twenty minutes later, Cameron had flour in his hair and egg on his shirt. He'd spilled sugar on the floor and had to sweep it up. His apron was smeared with chocolate splotches and butter stains.

Julia's apron was spotless and she hummed a perky tune as she briskly washed the bowls and utensils. What was wrong with this picture? Cameron shoved the broom into the utility closet as Julia turned the water off and dried her hands.

"As soon as the third batch is in the oven, I'll start the frosting." She dried one of the large bowls in preparation for the next step. "Maybe you can add the sprinkles at the end."

"Sprinkles?" He slammed the closet shut. "Now that's just demeaning."

Julia laughed. "You're so wrong. Sprinkles are a critical part of the operation."

"I'll show you a critical part," he said with a growl as he grabbed her from behind.

Her protest landed somewhere between a scream and a giggle. Then her eyes flared as Cameron managed to ease her blouse off, then handily relieved her of her blue jeans.

"What have you done?" she asked, glancing down at her pristine apron, which was all that remained of her clothing. It was still tied neatly at her waist. "How did you do that?"

He waved his hands. "Magic." Scanning her from head to toe, he said, "Very nice. Now turn around."

"I don't think so," she said, backing away from him.

He ripped his apron off and unbuttoned his

shirt as he stalked her. Her back hit the kitchen wall as the oven timer buzzed.

"Perfect timing," she said, and made a sideways move toward the oven.

Cameron held her in place. "Stay right there." He pulled the second batch of cupcakes out of the oven and placed them on a rack, then slipped the third batch in and set the timer for fifteen minutes.

"I have to start the frosting now," she said.

"Not yet." He pulled her close and turned to switch places with her, so now his back was against the wall. He slipped his hands under her apron and clutched her exposed backside, shaping it with both of his hands. "This is what every guy watching your baking demonstrations has been fantasizing all week."

"Don't be silly—oh," she said, her protest fading as he cupped her bottom and lifted her. She wrapped her legs around his waist and moaned as she sank onto his rigid length. "Oh, Cameron."

"I told you I knew my way around the kitchen."

* * *

Julia's conference ended two days later. Cameron enlisted the help of most of the bell-man staff to load up two cars with suitcases, Julia's kitchen equipment and the baby's gear. Then they caravanned back to Dunsmuir Bay.

Cameron pulled into the tree-lined driveway that led to his two-story, Craftsman-style home overlooking the cliffs and parked his Porsche next to the three-car garage. He jogged to Julia's minivan, slid opened the back door and stepped into the car to take Jake out of his car seat.

"We're home, buddy," he whispered as Julia gathered her purse and keys and climbed down from the driver's seat. "Hope you like it here."

Holding the baby, Cameron led Julia to the carved-oak door leading into his home. She stopped and gazed out at the wide lawn that rolled all the way to the cliffs overlooking Dunsmuir Bay.

"It's beautiful," she said, shielding the sun from her eyes.

"Yeah, it is," he said, staring at her as the baby bounced in his arms.

Julia felt her cheeks heat up from his intense gaze. She swallowed self-consciously. "I think we'll be very happy here."

"Good," he said, and kissed her. "Let's go inside."

"Okay."

Cameron swung the front door open, then stopped, blocking the entryway.

"Is something wrong?" she asked.

"Everything's perfect," he assured her, "but I want to do this right. You hold Jake, okay?"

Julia grabbed hold of the baby, then Cameron bent and lifted both her and the baby into his arms and carried them into his home. Once inside, he kissed her again. "Welcome home."

"Thank you," she whispered. "You can put us down now."

"Oh, yeah." He grinned and kissed her one last time, then gave the baby's forehead a smooch before letting them go.

As Cameron placed the baby in his rolling

bouncy chair, Julia gazed around, taking in the large living area. Peg-and-groove hardwood floors spanned the length of the room from the front door to the wide wall of glass on the opposite side. The ultra-modern kitchen was open to the room and the vaulted ceiling rose up two floors, making the space feel even bigger. Along one wall, the wide staircase led to the second floor.

Spacious rugs covered the living room area where several chairs and sofas were arranged to create a number of conversation areas. A riverstone hearth and fireplace was built into one wall, lending the room a warm, cozy feel despite its massive size.

"My housekeeper had everything baby-proofed, but we'll go through and double-check to make sure everything's extra safe for Jake."

"It's beautiful, Cameron," she said, making a beeline for the opposite end of the space where the dining room connected to the kitchen. She was curious to see where she would spend much of her time every day.

In the dining room, she stared through the thick glass wall at the ocean. There were white-caps on the water today and sailboats dotted the horizon. "Spectacular."

"And the view from the kitchen is just as nice."

*"Nice?"* she said, smiling as she checked out the fabulous views. The kitchen walls were painted a dark gold, maybe too dark for her taste, but that could be changed. "It's gorgeous. And huge. I can watch the waves crash while I bake. This place is a showcase."

He laughed. "Is that a genteel way of saying it's not exactly comfortable?"

"Are you kidding?" she asked, her eyes wide. "It's very comfortable. It's a real home."

"I like to think so." He glanced around the kitchen. "I spend most of my time in here or out by the pool. There's a den upstairs where I like to watch TV, although sometimes I'll use the set in the living room." He was rambling, she real-ized. Was he nervous? "Anyway, I hope you'll feel at home here."

"I already do." She wrapped her arms around

his waist and laid her head against his shoulder. After a moment, she leaned back and added, "Although it's awfully clean."

He raised an eyebrow. "Again that doesn't sound like a compliment."

"Oh, it is," she said laughing. "I'm just so used to the clutter of my old place. It's up in the hills and it's big and old. I love your home much more." *Because you're here,* she thought. And because this was a real home, not a mausoleum. She looked around some more, then grimaced. "I just hope you know what you're getting yourself into. With Jake here, your lovely clean home will deteriorate into a jumbled mass of toys and clutter."

"I can't wait," he insisted, and followed her back into the living room as she explored the space. "It'll be fun."

"No, I mean it," she said, strolling over to run her hand along the back of the dark gray sectional. "He's like a tornado."

"This place can handle it," Cameron said. "And if you don't like anything, we'll get rid of it.

I want you both to be happy and comfortable here. Believe me, I'm not tied to anything in this room."

She sighed. "I hope not, because Jake's stuff seems to multiply and take over rooms. It's scary."

Cameron laughed. "It's okay, Julia. It'll be an improvement from the way it is now."

She glanced around as the baby began to bounce and wiggle. "You mean, neat and clean?"

"*Too* neat and clean," he clarified. "I'm glad Jake's here to liven things up."

She shrugged and watched as the baby rolled and bounced his way across the Persian carpet. "Don't say I didn't warn you."

"That was a waste of three days," Brandon muttered as he slid into the back seat of the limousine and slammed the door shut.

Adam took off his sunglasses and slipped them in his pocket. "The first two days were worthwhile. It was just today that sucked."

"True," Cameron said with a nod. "But now we know who we're dealing with."

"Yeah," Brandon said. "Idiots."

The head of one of their subsidiaries, Jeremy Gray, had set up the meeting in Delaware earlier that morning, thinking the two companies might find enough common ground for a merger. It hadn't worked out, to say the least.

"I'm scheduling a meeting with Jeremy first thing tomorrow morning," Adam said, pulling out his cell phone. "I want to know what the hell he was thinking, setting this up. That group won't be ready to take their operation nationwide for another two years."

"If ever," Brandon added.

The rest of the drive from the airport was made in relative silence. Cameron was dropped off first and after grabbing his suitcase from the trunk, he thanked their driver and told his brothers he would see them in the morning.

He was tired but happy to be home. He'd always enjoyed traveling for business, but this time he had to admit he was beat. More than that, he'd actually missed his new family. It had been disconcerting to find himself in the middle of a business meeting, checking the time and wondering what Julia and Jake were doing right at that moment. He refused to read too much into his feelings, though, chalking it up to the fact that the newness of being part of a family hadn't worn off yet.

Stepping inside the house, he paused for a moment and listened for their voices. Then he took the stairs two at a time and found Julia in Jake's room, putting the baby to bed for the night. She whispered sweet nothings and rubbed Jake's stomach for a minute before winding up the colorful wizard mobile over his bed and wishing him sweet dreams.

Cameron leaned against the doorjamb, taking in the warm, homey scene. When Julia spied him, she let out a muted cry, then raced over and pulled him out into the hall where she wrapped herself around him. "I'm so glad you're home."

"Me, too." He breathed in the sultry scent of her.

"Do you want dinner?" she asked.

"No, I had something earlier at the airport. But I could go for a beer. Then bed."

They walked downstairs arm in arm. "What have you been up to while I was gone?"

"You'll see in a minute," she said, her tone lighthearted.

In the kitchen, he headed for the refrigerator, then stopped. He glanced around the room. It took him a few seconds before he realized what was different. "You painted my kitchen. And where's my refrigerator?"

She smiled brightly. "It's just a few shades lighter than it was, but it makes a nice change, don't you think? And your refrigerator is in the garage. We can still use it for storing drinks and frozen foods, but mine was practically brand-new and it's so much bigger and laid out better. I didn't think you'd mind."

He opened the new refrigerator to look for a bottle of beer. It took a minute before he found them stacked neatly along the door. He twisted the cap off and took a long drink. "You could've asked me."

Her smile dimmed. "It was a spur-of-the-moment decision. I guess I should've warned you, I make them sometimes. And you weren't here."

"You could've called."

"I didn't want to bother you while you were in meetings." She sniffed. "Besides, you made it clear you'd be too busy to talk much."

"We talked last night," he pointed out. "You could've told me then."

Her lips compressed in a tight frown. "We were discussing other things. I forgot."

*Oh yeah,* he thought, recalling the conversation. They'd had phone sex. He took another sip of beer, then muttered, "Well, next time let me know."

"Fine."

She sounded annoyed. *Join the club,* he thought, and tossed the bottle cap in the trash can, which she'd moved to the opposite side of the room, closer to the service porch. Irritated now, he said, "Look, just ask me before you make changes to my house."

"And here I thought it was *our* house now," she said as she wiped off Jake's high chair. "My mistake."

"I didn't mean it like that."

"No? Well, it sounded *like that*."

"Sorry, but I've had a long, frustrating day."

"And I haven't?"

"That's not my point."

"Oh, did you have a point?"

Yeah, she was definitely annoyed. But so was he. "I'm just saying that this is the kind of decision we should both have a hand in making."

"Fine." She threw the sponge down. "I'll call the painters and have them change it back to the way it was. Then we'll discuss it."

"Don't be ridiculous."

"Oh, now I'm being ridiculous?"

"Well, you're not making much sense," he said. "I'm just saying it's important for us to—"

"I'll tell you what's important," she said, wagging her finger in his face. "Me. That's what.

I'm important. And my work space is important. Call me a temperamental artist, but I need to enjoy the space I work in. And that means the kitchen. Your refrigerator wasn't efficient and the color of this room was too dark for me. I didn't feel creative, I didn't feel like it was mine. It sounds stupid, but it's true. So I changed the color and made it mine. Now I can work here. That's the bottom line. So live with it."

"I'm trying to live with it, Julia," he said, wrapping his hand around her finger to stop her from jabbing at him. "But don't expect me to roll over and let you change everything that's mine, just because you..." He hesitated.

"Oh, don't stop now," she said, inches from his face.

But he had to stop. *Everything that's mine,* he'd just said. Damn. She was right. His house was *their* house now. And she needed to feel comfortable here. He'd get used to the new refrigerator. And why did he care what color the kitchen walls were? He didn't, but Julia did. And looking around, he could see that it actually did look better, lighter, brighter in here now.

Besides, her scent was driving him nuts. Why were they fighting? He couldn't remember, but one thing was for certain. He was a fool to start a fight when he'd been traveling for seventy-two hours straight.

"Why don't you put stickers on anything that's yours," she continued angrily. "Never mind, we'll just assume *every*thing's yours."

He moved a half inch closer and took a deep breath. "You smell like flowers. And lemons."

"Don't change the subject," she chided, then added defensively, "I made lemonade."

His eyes narrowed in on her. "I like lemonade."

He had her cornered against the chrome door of the ultra-modern refrigerator. She tried to edge sideways. "I'm going to bed."

"Not yet." He held her shoulders to keep her close. "You forgot something."

"What?"

"This," he said, and kissed her, his mouth

taking hers in a rush of heat and an explosion of taste and need.

When she groaned, he lifted her up onto the counter. Sliding his hands up the insides of her thighs, he spread her legs. Then he pulled her closer to the edge and knelt before her.

"Cameron," she whispered.

"Shh," he said, then kissed the inside of her knee and moved higher, to her thighs, first one side, then the other. Hearing her moan in pleasure, he used his tongue to part her sensitive folds and plunged deeply. Her wild cry satisfied his masculine pride as he delved deeper, pressing his lips to her, sliding his mouth and tongue against her slick center, licking and suckling.

She was intoxicating. He couldn't get enough of her. When she screamed his name, he didn't wait a second longer. He stood and, watching her closely, unfastened his jeans, shoving them down his legs. Her eyes flashed at the sight of his impressive erection.

"Come to me," he said, lifting her up and onto

his stiff length and slowly lowering her until he filled her completely.

Her lusty sigh pushed him to the limit, but he forced himself to go slowly. At first. But she was so hot, so tight, so ready, that he began pumping into her with an urgency that brought him close to the edge of his control. Moments later, she cried out and he fused his lips to hers as he drove himself to join her in a climax so intense, he had to wonder if they might both go up in flames.

They leaned against the kitchen counter, holding on to each other like drunken sailors. Cameron wasn't ready to let her go just yet. He vaguely remembered fighting about something, but now it seemed nothing more than a prelude to some of the best sex he'd ever had.

"I might regret asking," she said, resting her head on his shoulder as she lazily stroked his back. "But I need to know what you're thinking right now."

He looked around, then met her gaze. "I was thinking I really like the new paint job."

\* \* \*

After the kitchen confrontation and its pleasurable aftermath, Cameron and Julia settled into a routine. He was amazed at how easily the three of them were adjusting to life together in his home.

Even though there were staff bakers at her store doing the yeoman's work of making the products she sold every day, Julia liked to bake her signature delicacies at home. She was up early every morning, kneading and mixing and baking and frosting, so Cameron got into the habit of joining her.

"Almost like a real marriage," he muttered, and caught himself wincing at the words. This wasn't what he'd had in mind when they entered into this arrangement.

He hadn't counted on caring about her so much.

And it was getting more and more difficult to keep from letting his feelings show.

"I can't believe my kid likes carrots for breakfast," Cameron said, looking baffled as he fed Jake another spoonful of pureed carrots.

"He likes everything." Julia poured herself another cup of coffee.

"Yeah, but carrots? Go figure." He loaded another bit of carrot mixture onto Jake's spoon, then turned as a thought occurred. "Maybe we should start a vegetable garden."

"Good idea," she murmured. Her eyes widened. "A vegetable garden? With carrots. Oh, my God, carrots and carrots." She grabbed the pad and pen by the telephone and scribbled a note.

"Well, we could have other stuff, too." Cameron shrugged as he lifted the spoon up in the air and made like an airplane toward Jake's mouth. "Cucumbers, tomatoes, lettuce, maybe some different kinds of peppers."

She put down the pen and sat forward. "No, carats, like diamonds and rubies. And carrots. And tomatoes and cucumbers. A garden. For kids. And a museum for the diamonds and the art and, oh, everything. That's it."

"That's what?"

She jumped up and planted a kiss on Cameron's lips. "You're brilliant."

"I've always thought so," he said, flashing her a look of puzzled amusement as she ran out of the room.

Upstairs in the room Cameron had reconfigured to be her home office, Julia powered up her computer and began to write out a short proposal for the Parrish Trust board of directors.

She had always planned to open her family home to the public one day. It was too big, too magnificent and too full of her parents' rare and beautiful art, furnishings and books to keep to herself. But she'd also wanted to leave her own mark, provide something memorable, something different, something *important* to people. To children.

It sounded simplistic that a vegetable garden might be that important mark, but Julia loved the idea. It would bring children to Glen Haven Farm. Of course, this wouldn't be a simple vegetable garden. It would be huge, a community garden with terraced beds. There would be animals, maybe a petting zoo, definitely a barn, classrooms, field trips, picnics, fun. While children had fun in the garden, their parents could tour the Parrish Museum and Library.

She spent most of the morning brainstorming her idea before enlisting Cameron's help to pull it all together.

He sat quietly while she made her presentation. When she asked for his thoughts and reactions, the first thing he said was, "Why?"

"Why?" she repeated. "What do you mean?"

"I mean, I get the garden idea. But why would you want to turn your home into a museum?"

Confused at first, she eventually understood his question. "You've never been to my home."

He shook his head. "Not yet."

She'd used a moving company to transport the bits of furniture, clothing and personal items she and Jake had needed when they moved into Cameron's home. It had all been arranged in a day and Cameron had been at work the whole time. She'd never taken him up to her house, so of course he had no idea what it looked like.

She leaned back and gazed up at him. "If you

have an extra few hours today, I'd love to show you where I grew up."

"I'd like that, too," he said, kissing the soft skin of her neck. "A little later." Then he took hold of her hand and led her upstairs.

Three weeks later, on a breezy Saturday afternoon, Cameron held Jake in his arms as he and Julia stood on the smooth stone steps in front of Glen Haven Farm, Julia's family home—or, as she liked to call it, the Mausoleum.

To call the place a farm was patently absurd, Cameron thought, since the elegant residence and finely manicured grounds had been designed and built in the grand style of a Regency estate.

The home itself was a three-story mansion with four separate wings extending out from what Julia called the central gallery. *Gallery* was the perfect word for it. There was priceless artwork everywhere, paintings on every wall, costly porcelain and silver pieces on every surface, and stately antique furniture in every room.

Julia's brainstorm had been spot on, Cameron thought now. The place was made to be a museum. But that wasn't what had excited her. No, she'd been trying to find a way to bring children to the house. Artwork wouldn't do it, but a huge vegetable garden would. Kids could grow and harvest their own vegetables and have fun while they learned some healthy lessons. Julia had whipped up a business plan in no time flat and scheduled a trustees' meeting to go over her ideas.

On Cameron's first tour of the place a few weeks earlier, Julia had mentioned casually that the main residence was more than thirty thousand square feet. The lawns, gardens, pools, rare trees, bowered rose garden and other botanical delights comprised ninety acres of prime real estate overlooking Dunsmuir Bay.

With Sally Duke as his adoptive mother, Cameron had grown up with money and luxury, but this was something else. To be honest, Cameron couldn't help thinking that this amazing house, with its massive grounds and stunning views, would make one hell of a Duke resort.

But this was Julia's show, and it was now show-time.

"Thank you for being here with me," she whispered to Cameron as they watched a stretch limousine wind its way up the long driveway.

"Wouldn't miss it for the world," he said. As he dipped down to kiss her cheek, he added, "I've got your back."

The limo driver parked and four older men in dark suits climbed out. As they approached, Julia grabbed Cameron's hand. He could feel the nervous energy coursing through her.

Why his strong, independent wife felt she needed backup was a mystery to him. After all, this was her home, her decision. Not only that, but it was her money, her heritage. So who cared what these fat cats thought? Apparently, Julia did.

As the four men came closer, Julia smiled and patted Jake's butt for luck, then strolled over to greet the trustees. Cameron handed the baby over to the nanny, who took Jake inside. Then he followed Julia and greeted two of the lawyers he recognized from past business deals around town.

"So, Duke," said Dave Saunders, an overfed blowhard Cameron had never liked, "why aren't you turning this place into one of your fancy hotels?"

"Who says I'm not?" he said pleasantly.

The four men exchanged glances and Cameron earned a skeptical look from Julia. He winked at her as if to urge her not to take any of this too seriously.

So these were the four almighty trustees Julia believed were in charge of her destiny. No wonder she thought she needed backup.

After the introductions were made, Julia led the entire group across the wide lawn to the first of many spots on the property for which she had plans.

As a light breeze stirred the leaves, the men stopped to gaze up at what looked like a smaller version of the ancient Greek Acropolis built into the hillside.

One of the men chuckled. "Ah, the famous Glen Haven Folly."

"Seems a waste of good real estate," Saunders mused.

"And money," a third man added with a significant nod to the others.

"My father had it built for me when I studied ancient Greece in third grade," Julia explained briefly.

One of the men sniffed. Another muttered, "Must be nice."

Cameron stifled the urge to smack the guy upside his head.

Julia ignored the sarcasm and pointed forward. "Now we continue along this path to the western end of the meadow."

As they passed an old wrought-iron gate built into an ivy-covered stone wall, Cameron stopped to look through the gateway. He hadn't noticed it on his first visit. Inside the thick wall, row after row of tall hedges were aligned in a circular pattern that covered a wide stretch of green lawn. Intrigued, he took another, closer look.

"Whoa, is that a maze?"

Julia stopped and turned. "Yes."

"That's incredible," he exclaimed. "You grew up with a maze in your backyard?"

She glanced over her shoulder and saw that the four men had stopped to wait for them.

"Now what?" said Harold Greer, the oldest trustee.

Cameron smiled. "We'll just be a minute, gentlemen."

Glaring at Cameron, Julia said, "Yes, it's a maze."

He pulled her closer to the gate and peered through. "This is amazing. Is there anything in the middle?"

She sighed. "A life-size chess set."

Cameron turned. "You've got a life-size chess set in the middle of the maze?"

"That's right," she said defensively.

"With life-size chess pieces? Like French royalty or something?"

"Or something," she said through clenched teeth.

"French royalty, they wish," one of the other trustees muttered.

"It's shrubbery, Duke," Dave Saunders said with a sneer. "Get over it."

Greer sighed. "Miss Parrish, is this going to take all day?"

Julia cringed. "I'm so sorry, Mr. Greer."

Cameron's eyes narrowed. From her tone and the surreptitious looks she'd been sending the tight-assed trustees for the past half hour, this wasn't the first time she'd felt the need to either defend or recoil from her late parents' supposed profligate style. And right then he wished she'd never set up this meeting. He wanted to sweep her up and carry her away from their hypercritical opinions and high-handedness.

In his years of dealing with these kinds of guys, Cameron had learned not to take them too seriously, especially when he was the one holding the purse strings. But Julia had grown up under the control of people like these men.

They'd been in charge, running her life, making decisions. As strong as he knew her to be, she'd clearly never stood up to these men before. No wonder she was nervous.

"Excuse us for just a moment, gentlemen," he said, then took hold of her hand and pulled her away, back around the bend of the thick wall.

"What do you think you're doing?" she asked in a furious whisper.

After checking to make sure they were far enough away not to be overheard by the trustees, Cameron said, "Why are you trying so hard to impress these guys?"

"Their opinions are important."

"They work for you," he said, pointing at her. "They should be trying to impress you so they keep their jobs, but they're not. What's going on here?"

Her chest rose and fell slowly. "It's not that simple, Cameron."

"It *is* that simple," he said. "These guys have no say over your decisions."

She shifted uncomfortably. "Yes, but they've

worked for my family trust for years. If they think I'm spending money unwisely…"

"You're not," he insisted.

"And you're not helping," she added irately, folding her arms across her chest. "Going on and on about the maze and the stupid chess set. What was that all about? I need you to focus."

"Trust me, I'm completely focused on the thought of chasing you naked through that maze."

"Cameron." Flustered, she peered around to see if he'd been overheard. "I'm trying to be professional here. These guys have never thought of me as anything but a frivolous trust-fund baby. Maybe I don't need their support exactly, but I would like to have their respect."

"Respect?" He frowned. It hadn't ever occurred to him that his wife wouldn't be respected anywhere she went. And that thought just pissed him off. "Okay, I'm going to share some insider information that I think will put everything into perspective for you."

She scowled. "Oh, this should be good."

"I don't offer this sort of strategy to everyone, you know."

"Just get on with it." She tapped her foot. "They're waiting for us."

"Let them wait," he said, then lowered his voice. "I've known Dave Saunders for years. I went to college with him and I've done business deals with his firm. If he has two drinks, he starts taking his clothes off and dancing. The guy's got a gut on him that won't quit, and he's a bad dancer. Overbite, little fist pumps, the whole deal."

She smothered a laugh. "Stop it."

"I'm serious here. Just do me a favor—the next time he dismisses your opinion or makes you feel less than amazing, I want you to picture him in his baggy underwear, doing the hully gully. It's not pretty. Will you promise me you'll do that?"

"I hope it never comes to that," she said solemnly as she tried to suppress another giggle.

"I hope not, too. But this is a tried-and-true business strategy. You'll thank me for it later."

She gazed at him, then gave him a quick hug. "Thank you."

"No problem." He jerked his head toward the trustees. "Go give 'em hell."

Taking a deep breath, she said, "I suppose you're going to want to check out the maze after this."

His eyebrows shot up. "You know I am."

She cocked her head to look up at him. "And I bet you'd never get lost in a maze, would you?"

"Not a chance."

"I didn't think so." She paused, then her eyes glittered with determination. "So he's got the overbite going and everything?"

"Oh, yeah."

With a quick nod, she said, "Thanks. I appreciate it."

"Like I said, I've got your back."

Cameron watched as she composed herself, then turned and rejoined the trustees. She had once told him that she refused to play the poor little rich girl, but Cameron hadn't known the half of it. She'd come from one of the richest families in the state, but she'd grown up lonely and starved for affection, living on a massive estate with no one to talk to but the hired help.

And she'd had to deal with snot-nosed lawyers like these guys her whole life. Men who thought they knew more than she did about everything. But they couldn't be more wrong.

As Julia showed the trustees where she planned to plant the half-acre vegetable garden and the spot she thought would be perfect for a barn and petting zoo, Cameron realized he was going to have a good time watching her prove just how wrong they could be.

It had been several weeks since the meeting with the trustees. Julia had turned the museum plans over to a project management company, and while she still kept an eye on things at Glen Haven Farm, she was finally able to return to her early-morning baking schedule. The nanny showed up every morning in time for Julia and Cameron to go off to work. Some days, Cameron worked in his office at home, and on those days,

Julia came home early and gave the nanny the afternoon off.

One afternoon, Julia arrived to find the house empty. It was sunny and warm, so she followed her instincts and walked through the kitchen to the sliding door that led out to the patio. Sure enough, her two men were in the pool.

Cameron was holding on to Jake who was wrapped securely in a bright yellow life jacket decorated with cartoon characters.

"Ready?" Cameron asked.

"Da-da-da-da!" Jake blubbered excitedly.

"One, two, three," Cameron shouted, then bounced Jake on the water, causing a wave to form and splash against his daddy. Jake shrieked with laughter.

Julia laughed, too. The wave was tiny, but Cameron pretended to be drenched in water to make Jake laugh. Her two men looked so adorable together, her heart was in danger of melting.

Was it possible to be more in love than she already was?

"Oh, no," she whispered. Her knees were

suddenly weak, so she backed up and slid into the nearest patio chair. Her eyes began to tear up. It was just the bright sunlight, she thought. There was no way she could possibly be in love with Cameron Duke.

Oh, of course, she *loved* him. That was inevitable. But she couldn't be *in love* with him. That would ruin everything.

Dear God, how could she be so stupid? Staring at Cameron playing with Jake in the pool, she had to admit to herself that it wasn't all that hard.

"Don't be ridiculous," she retorted aloud. That was lust, pure and simple, and nothing more. The man was capable of turning her on with a wink of his eye. Didn't mean she was in love with him.

Hadn't she worked all this out at the wedding? All they had was a marriage of convenience. Falling in love was *not* convenient. It wasn't part of the plan.

So why was her heart beating so fast? Why were her knees so weak? Maybe she was coming down with the flu. Anything but the alternative.

Jake's little screams of delight kept her anchored as her mind spun out of control. She needed to reel it back in, now. Because it couldn't work. Cameron would never reciprocate her feelings, so why would she endanger their relationship by insisting that he do just that?

She wouldn't. Even if it meant lying through her teeth, she would never admit that she was in love with her husband. And didn't that sound absurd?

"I'm going to make lemonade," she said, waving to Cameron and Jake before going inside. As she cut lemons and began to squeeze out the juice, she watched through the window as Jake giggled at Cameron's antics. He really was the best father, she thought.

She recalled the diamond necklace Cameron had given her while they were still at the hotel, to thank her for agreeing to marry him. Then the night they'd moved into his house, he'd slipped a matching diamond bracelet on her wrist.

Was it dangerous to read anything into the fact that he gave her lovely gifts whenever wonderful

things happened in his life? It had already occurred to her that this wasn't about the jewelry.
It had to be something more than just a gesture.
His gifts always seemed to come from a warm,
loving place within him. Within his heart. Was
it Cameron's way of telling her he loved her?

"Oh, there you go again," she said irately,
pounding half a lemon onto the juicer and
squeezing it to within an inch of its life. "Snap
out of it."

Cameron Duke took care of what was his. She
was his wife; Jake was his son. Cameron would
do whatever it took to keep them healthy and
happy. He would protect them with his life and
make them feel as if they were the most important people in the world. Which made him all
the more special to her. If that meant she was a
sap, so be it.

Julia sighed as she added sugar and stirred it
into the mixture of water and juice. Was it any
wonder that she'd fallen in love with the man?
Now she would just have to keep that realization
hidden deep within her heart so that Cameron

would never learn the truth. Because Cameron Duke would never allow love to be a part of his plan.

# Nine

"It looks like they're going to catch on fire," Julia said in a worried tone.

Cameron and his brothers stood around the barbecue grill cooking sausages, burgers and steaks. They didn't seem to notice the billowing clouds of smoke that enveloped them as they laughed and talked and drank beer.

"But they never do, honey," Sally said dryly as she placed folded cloth napkins and plates on the patio table. "It's a male ritual. Don't try to make sense of it."

"Don't be too concerned, Julia," Trish said,

stopping to give her new sister-in-law's shoulder a comforting pat before continuing to add utensils and glassware to each place setting. "You won't have to worry about Jake joining them in the manly smoke, at least for another year or two."

Julia shuddered and stroked Jake's head, then sprinkled a handful of Cheerios onto the tray of his bouncy chair. They had been living with Cameron for two months now, and Cameron had decided to celebrate the milestone with their first official family barbecue.

The late spring day was sunny and warm, so they'd all spent quality time in the pool before starting dinner. Everyone had dried off and changed into shorts, shirts and flip-flops. Sally, with her blond hair pulled back in a neat ponytail, sipped Julia's homemade sangria.

Julia had baked hot dog and hamburger buns that morning and now she placed the large, plastic-wrapped cookie sheet on the sunny side table near the grill.

Sally shook her head at the sheet full of buns.

"Now I know you're a baker, but it still amazes me that you baked these yourself just for us."

"Of course I did," Julia said. "They're so easy." She glanced back at the buns on the table. "I'm hoping the sunshine will warm them instead of sticking them in the oven. What do you think?"

"I think that's a stroke of genius," Trish said. She finished with the utensils and picked up her glass of fizzy water. "I would beg you for the recipe, but why? My new sister-in-law owns a bakery."

They all laughed. "I'll bake them for you personally anytime you want."

"Don't tempt me," Trish said.

Julia headed for the sliding glass door leading to the kitchen. "Anyone for more sangria?"

"I'd love a glass," Sally said.

"None for me, thanks," Trish said easily. "It's not good for the baby."

Sally leaned over the table to straighten a fork, but froze in mid-move. She turned and stared at her daughter-in-law. "No."

"Yes," Trish said, her laugh filled with joy.

"Oh." The older woman's eyes misted as she clasped her hand over her mouth in shock and wonder.

Julia felt her own eyes dampen, as well. "You're having a baby?"

Trish nodded, still grinning.

Sally grabbed Trish in a warm hug. "Oh, I'm so happy."

"That's wonderful," Julia said, and laughed as she joined in the hug fest. In that instant, her heart was so full of love for these two women and the baby yet to be born. She couldn't begin to describe how grateful she was to be a part of this family and this thrilling moment.

Sally covered her face and began to cry in earnest. "I'm just overwhelmed. And overjoyed. I never thought…and then Julia and Jake came into our lives, and now Trish, and a baby, and… Oh, will you look at me, carrying on?"

"It's wonderful," Julia said, sniffling.

Trish and Julia linked arms with their mother-in-law and they all put their heads together.

"This is the most fantastic day ever," Sally

whispered, then her eyes lit up. "And little Jake will have a cousin to grow up with."

Julia sniffed as tears began to flow again. "Oh, great. Now you've got me going again."

Sally patted both of their cheeks. "You girls are both such a gift."

Seconds later, Cameron walked over and saw Julia sniffle and wipe her eyes. He peered at her, then noticed his mother was crying, too. Alarmed, he grabbed Julia's arm. "What's wrong? You're all crying. What happened? Is it Jake?"

"No, no," Julia said quickly, then laughed. "It's good news. It's Trish. She's going to have a baby."

He broke out into a grin, turned and pulled Trish close for a big hug. He kissed her right on the lips and said, "That's great news, honey."

"Thanks, Cameron," she said, smiling.

He jogged back to the grill and punched his brother in the arm. Then he gave him a brisk hug.

"What's up?" Brandon asked.

"They're having a baby," Cameron explained.

Brandon choked on his beer, and Cameron thumped his back. When he'd recovered fully, Brandon grabbed Adam in a bear hug. "Congratulations, man."

Adam laughed. "Thanks."

The three brothers clicked their beer bottles together in a toast just as Sally rushed over to give Adam a ferocious hug.

"Lots of hugs going on around here," Cameron said.

Sally turned and said, "I just can't help it." Then she hugged Adam again. "Oh, sweetie. I'm so happy for you."

"Thanks, Mom," Adam said, unable to conceal his grin of masculine satisfaction.

"Glad he's not shooting blanks?" Brandon said wryly.

"Oh, you," Sally said, and smacked his arm lightly. "Just wait till it's your turn."

"Whoa. Threats?" Brandon gave her an incredulous look. "Sorry, Mom, but you'll be waiting a long time for that day."

"We'll see about that," Sally muttered, then gave him a pointed look before turning back to join the girls.

Brandon's shoulders shook violently and he glanced at his brothers. "Did anyone else feel that sudden chill?"

"Yeah, I saw that look she gave you," Cameron said, his lips twisted in a wry grin. "I'd say you're screwed."

Brandon glared from one brother to the other. "Whatever happened to our sacred vows? We made a pact. Blood brothers forever, remember?"

"We're still blood brothers," Adam said amiably, then took a long sip of beer. "Always will be."

"Yeah, but come on," Brandon groused. "First, there's your marriage. I could almost handle that. But then Cameron went and did it. That blew my mind, I've gotta tell you. And now, more kids?"

"Stuff happens," Cameron said by way of explanation. What else could he say? He couldn't figure it out, either.

Brandon shook his head. "And now I'll have Mom on my case, bellyaching for me to do the same. And that's never going to happen."

"You think not?" Adam said.

"Never," Brandon said decisively, and pointed his beer bottle at both of them. "I understand you two are feeble-minded amateurs when it comes to women, but I'm a professional. I've got standards to uphold."

Adam threw back his head and howled with laughter. "Standards. That's a good one, bro."

"Yeah." Cameron patted Brandon's back. He understood standards. They were a lot like rules. Sometimes both were meant to be broken. "Lots of luck with those standards."

"You guys are killing me," Brandon muttered, then slugged down the rest of his beer. "Getting so you can't trust anyone anymore."

"Why don't you just tell him how you feel?" Karolyn asked as she filled the refrigerated display case with more freshly wrapped sandwiches from the Cupcake kitchen.

"I don't know what you're talking about," Julia said. She grabbed a large tub from the busboy tray behind the checkout counter. "Lynnie took a break so I'm going to bus the tables out front."

"You're avoiding the conversation," Karolyn whispered.

"Yes," she admitted. "But I'm working, too."

Karolyn rolled her eyes and went back to tucking and folding the small, white boxes used by customers to carry home their bakery goods. The word Cupcake was embossed in navy blue on the top, under the outline of a fluffy cupcake.

The white box and the navy-blue ribbon tie had become an iconic symbol in Dunsmuir Bay. When mothers arrived home carrying a Cupcake box, children turned into angels. When the boss showed up at the office with a Cupcake box, it was better than getting a promotion.

Julia stacked empty latte cups, pastry plates and utensils in the tub, then wiped down the tables. She greeted three of her customers who always met here for lattes and a snack after their morning workout, then answered a question about the sandwich special of the day.

Glancing around the café area, she assured herself that everything was clean and tidy. She was proud of what she'd created here. Even before her customers walked inside, they could smell the mouth-watering aroma of baked bread, puff pastry and sweet chocolate chip cookies all the way down the street.

Julia returned the filled tub to the busboy tray behind the counter just as Lynnie finished her break.

"Julia," Karolyn called from the kitchen. "Can you come back and check on the cheese bread?"

Julia made sure Lynnie was ready to work and checked that her young assistant's apron was tied securely to cover the tacky saying on her T-shirt before walking into the kitchen. Karolyn grabbed her arm and pulled her all the way to the back door leading to the tiny, fenced-in patio.

"Now, sit," Karolyn said.

Julia glanced around at the colorful flower boxes and miniature potted lemon trees that decorated the space. "No cheese-bread emergency?"

"No."

With a slow, heavy exhalation, Julia sat at the small table they'd set up for staff meetings and coffee breaks. "All right. What do you want?"

Karolyn pulled another chair around to get closer. She grabbed Julia's hand and squeezed it. "I'm worried about you."

"I'm perfectly fine," Julia countered breezily. "Business is booming. I'm married to a gorgeous man who is a terrific father. We have a wonderful life. Cameron loves Jake, and it's so sweet to see them together. He treats me like a princess. He's sexy and attentive and warm, and I'm...I'm happy."

"Honey," Karolyn said, shaking her hand to get her attention. "Don't you think he deserves to know you're in love with him?"

"Oh, God." Julia dropped her chin to her chest in defeat. "I never should've told you why we really got married."

"I'm your best friend. Who else can you share your deepest, darkest, dumbest secrets with?"

"True," she mumbled. "But why do you think I'm in love with him?"

"It's only written all over your face. *All* the time," Karolyn said. "Even Lynnie made a comment the other day, and you know she doesn't notice anything unless it's dressed in black leather and pierced in twenty-seven places."

Julia laughed, then sobered immediately. "What, exactly, did Lynnie notice?"

"That you're humming all the time, that your eyes have taken on a dreamy glow, that you leave early now. You never used to leave early." Karolyn leaned close and whispered, "She thinks you're in deep."

"Of course I leave early," Julia said, pouting at the idea that she was so transparent, even her employees were starting to notice. "I have a baby at home."

"That never stopped you from working all hours before." Karolyn grinned. "And you still have a devoted nanny who will stay all night with Jake if you need her to."

"Oh, God, even Lynnie noticed." Julia laid her head on the table. "That's pitiful."

"Sad but true," Karolyn said.

"What am I going to do?"

"You're going to go home and tell him you love him," Karolyn instructed. "And if he's got any guts at all, he'll tell you the same."

Julia stared forlornly at her friend. "He doesn't love me, Karolyn."

Karolyn laughed. "Oh, Julia."

Julia blinked. "It's not funny."

"Honey, he's so in love with you, it's ridiculous."

"No, he's not."

"I saw him at the wedding. He was smitten then, and it's even worse now."

Julia pursed her lips in discontent. "He wants me, I know that. But *want* isn't love."

Karolyn sighed. "Every time he walks into the bakery, the air becomes charged with electricity between you two."

Julia shook her head. "That's just lust."

"You can ignore the signs, and he might deny it to kingdom come, but take my word for it, Cameron Duke is a man who's in love with his wife."

The following Friday, Sally babysat Jake so that Julia and Cameron could attend a hotel-owners conference at Monarch Dunes.

Unlike her last visit when she had Jake with her, plus her own conference to attend, plus a wedding to organize, Julia was able to relax. Cameron made sure of it by arranging for her to spend the time being pampered at the hotel spa while he attended meetings. Julia couldn't remember the last time she'd spent a day in such luxury, with a mani-pedi, a facial and a massage. By the time she dressed for the owners' annual charity ball that evening, she felt completely fluffed and refreshed.

She blew her hair out straight so she could wear it up in a sleek, smooth style, instead of her usual loose waves. After stepping into the strapless burgundy gown Trish had helped her shop for, she fastened the gleaming diamond necklace around her neck and slipped on the matching bracelet. She'd brought her mother's diamond studs to wear in her ears.

Checking herself in the mirror one last time, Julia took a deep breath and walked out to the living room. There she saw Cameron, dressed in the elegant tuxedo he'd worn at their wedding, pop open the champagne and fill two glasses with bubbly gold liquid.

"That looks wonderful," she said. Whether she was referring to the frothy champagne or her husband, she couldn't say, but both were true.

He turned to hand her the glass, then stopped. And stared. The fiery intensity she saw in his eyes left shivers on her skin and heated up her insides.

"Wow," he said on an exhalation.

She smiled, delighted by his reaction. "Thank you."

"No, thank you," he murmured, and touched

his glass to hers. "Let's pass on the party and stay here."

"Aren't you the host of this thing?"

He grimaced. "Okay, we'll stay half an hour."

"Just long enough to dance one slow dance," she said, and sipped her champagne.

"We can do that right here," he said, taking her in his arms and swaying in place. After a moment, he chuckled. "You'd never know it from this, but I was actually forced to attend cotillion at an early age."

She gasped. "So was I."

"And we both survived," he said, grinning at her.

She laid her head on his shoulder. After a moment she whispered, "Mmm, you're a very good dancer."

"It's easy, with you in my arms," he said, as he planted slow kisses along her neck. "I didn't think you could possibly be more beautiful, but tonight you are."

Julia looked up at him, at his eyes smoldering with need, and felt her heart tremble. If she told him she'd fallen in love with him, what would he do? Would he be shocked? Angry that she'd broken the rules? Could he admit the same back to her? Staring at him now, Julia wondered if it was only wishful thinking, or could she really see her feelings reflected in his eyes?

"We'd better go now or we'll never leave the room," Cameron said gruffly. "And don't get too friendly with anyone at the party. We'll be in and out of there in thirty minutes."

As they moved through the party, greeting friends and business competitors, Cameron kept Julia's hand gripped in his. She was so stunning, every man in the room had their eyes on her. No way would he let her loose in this crowd of sharks.

"There's the man of the hour," someone said.

Cameron turned and grinned at his old friend Byron Mirabelle, owner of the prestigious Pinnacle Hotels chain. The two men exchanged hearty handshakes and Cameron introduced him to Julia. "Byron specializes in small, luxury hotels in the mountain states of Colorado, Wyoming and Montana."

"Got one going up near Park City, Utah, next year," the older man said proudly.

"That's fantastic," Cameron said. To Julia, he added, "Byron was one of my first mentors in the business."

"It's so nice to meet you," Julia said.

"And you're just the lady I've been wanting to meet," Byron said, and pointed his finger at Julia in accusation.

"Me?"

"Yes, you," Byron said jovially. "You're the reason my wife won't stay anywhere else but the Duke resorts when we're in California."

"But I'm…" Julia shot Cameron a look of puzzlement, then stared at Byron. "Why?"

Byron slipped his arm through hers. "Because of those chocolate croissants you make for the Dukes. We can't get them anywhere else."

"Oh, that's so sweet." Julia laughed as she patted his arm.

Byron leaned closer. "Personally, I'm partial

to your apple fritters. My goodness, I could eat them all day long." He frowned and slapped his gut a few times. "I think it shows."

"I like those best, too," she confided.

As Cameron watched his stunning wife interact with his friend, he felt a wave of tenderness so overwhelming he almost stumbled backward. Suddenly, his chest felt so full of emotion, he could hardly breathe.

What the hell was that?

Was he having a heart attack? He didn't think so. He wasn't in pain. Quite the opposite, in fact. He felt warm, fulfilled, happy. Bizarre.

Hell, he didn't know what was going on, but he knew he needed to move.

He left Julia and Byron chatting while he walked to the bar and ordered a shot of good Scotch. As he sipped the drink, he decided the best thing to do right now was to get Julia and slip out of here, take her back to the room and make love. And tomorrow, he couldn't wait to drive home and see Jake. He didn't know when it had happened, but he'd become a family man, and Julia and Jake had become the most important part of his life.

Cameron felt someone touch his shoulder and he turned.

"Hello, Cameron."

His back went rigid. "Martina."

"Don't you look handsome," she said, her voice as sultry as he remembered. She wore a black-lace dress that barely covered her impressive cleavage, which she used to great advantage by leaning close to him as she batted her eyes. "I was hoping I'd see you here tonight."

Cameron gazed at her with detachment. He had loved Martina once, or so he'd thought. Now, he looked at her and felt…nothing.

"So, where's Andrew?" he asked. And more important, where the hell was Julia? He peered over the heads of the crowd, trying to see where his wife and Byron had disappeared to.

Martina's lips curled in a pout. "Andrew's not coming. It's just as well. I've missed you, Cameron. How have you been?"

"Couldn't be better," he said tersely.

"Oh, I'm glad." She walked her fingers up the lapel of his tuxedo. "To be honest, I was hoping I'd find you here alone. Maybe you and I could go somewhere and…and talk, or perhaps…"

"Or perhaps what?" he said, and carefully removed her hand from his jacket. "Perhaps cheat on your husband? Make him jealous? I don't think so."

"Oh, Cameron, don't be bitter," she said, and gripped his arm. "I—I can't pretend anymore. Andrew and I are divorcing."

"Sorry to hear it." He didn't look at her, but instead continued to scan the room, searching for Julia.

"I think you should know," Martina said in a low voice. "The reason we broke up is I…I've never gotten over you, Cameron. I want you back."

He choked on a laugh. "That's rich."

"There you are," Julia said brightly, touching his shoulder. "Byron's such a doll. Oh, hello."

With some relief, Cameron turned and wrapped

his arm around his lovely wife. "Martina, this is my wife, Julia."

"Your…what?" Martina opened her mouth, then shut it. A wise choice.

"Hello, Martina," Julia said graciously, though Cameron could feel the tension in her body. She had to have seen the other woman hanging on to him.

"How do you do?" Martina said coolly, but Cameron saw two red spots appear on her cheeks. He'd seen her get angry before and knew the signs.

He leaned closer to Julia and whispered, "I think our half hour is up."

"All right," she said, then smiled at Martina. "Nice to meet you."

"Yeah, same here." Martina did an about-face and faded into the crowd.

Julia gazed up at him. "A friend?"

"Hardly," he said. "Let's get out of here."

They took the long way back to their suite, walking along the beach. It was a typical, late-spring evening in California and a mild breeze tickled Julia's skin. The tide was out and the waves lapped softly on the shore. She carried her heels in her hand and waited for the right moment to ask Cameron about Martina, the woman he'd been talking to. Julia had heard the last of their conversation. She knew the woman wanted him back.

Her words had sent dreadful chills of fear down Julia's spine. But then Cameron had laughed at Martina, and Julia could only hope that tonight would be the last they would ever see of the woman and her imposing cleavage.

"Let's go this way," Cameron said, taking her hand and guiding her to the stairs that led up to the hotel. When they reached the top, he veered off the path toward a large grove of trees. As they got closer, she heard water rushing.

"Is that the waterfall?"

"Yes," he said, pointing. "It's over by those trees."

She squeezed his hand. "Let's find it."

Clouds moved in the night sky, revealing a

full moon as they wandered through the forested area. After a few minutes, they came to a rock-covered hill. Carved into the base was a small, stone-lined pool. Water cascaded over the smooth boulders and splashed into the pool, which was lit from under the surface, giving the water a mystical blue glow.

"It's beautiful, like a tropical lagoon," she said, and gazed up at him. "Can we go in?"

Touching her cheek, he smiled at her. "I was hoping you'd want to."

She angled her head to catch a glimpse of something across the pool. "It looks like there's light coming from behind the waterfall."

"That's the grotto." He grinned and pulled her close. "It's every man's fantasy. Want to see it?"

Shooting him a dubious look, she said, "Do I want to see every man's fantasy? I'm not sure."

With a laugh, he ran his hands up and down her arms. "It's really just a spa, but it's awesome. Secluded, warm and well-lit."

"How do we get there?"

His lips curved up. "We swim."

She laughed nervously. Glancing around the smooth rock terrace, she saw a wide chaise longue with towels and bathrobes laid out. "Are those for us?"

"Yes."

"Will anyone see us?"

"No," he said confidently. "I've made sure of it."

That brought a smile to her face and her shyness disappeared. "Then let's go swimming."

He kissed her bare shoulder as he reached for the zipper of her gown and slowly lowered it. "I want to make love with you."

She shivered from his touch. "I want that, too."

"Are you cold?"

"Not at all."

"Good." He let go of the burgundy silk and it slid down her body. She stepped out of the dress and Cameron picked it up and draped it over a chair. He turned and stared at her in her high heels, a red thong and matching red strapless bra.

"You take my breath away."

She closed her eyes on a sigh. "Touch me, please."

He complied, but took his time, first running his hands down her spine, up her arms, then down again, shaping her hips and thighs lightly with his fingers. He stood behind her, kissing her neck and back as he moved his hands over the soft skin of her stomach. He stopped to toy with her tiny, jewel-encrusted belly ring, then his hands glided up to skim the sides of her sensitive breasts.

She groaned. "Cameron, I need…"

"I know, baby. I need that, too." His hands molded her breasts and he used his thumbs to massage her responsive nipples to a hard peak. When she moaned, he unlatched her bra and let it fall. She writhed in his arms as he pressed his hard length against her lower back. Then, turning her, he knelt and slowly slipped off her thong before parting her thighs.

"Oh," she gasped, as he kissed her inner thigh. He brushed his lips against her most sensitive skin, then used his tongue to touch her deeply.

She was trembling with desire, didn't think she could take any more, when he stood abruptly and lifted her in his arms.

"We'll swim later," he growled, and gently laid her down on the soft chaise. Watching Cameron rip off his jacket and shirt, Julia experienced a moment of potent clarity as she realized her feminine power. It was exhilarating to watch him peel off his trousers to reveal his enormous erection.

She held up her arms to welcome him. He knelt on the chaise and paused to slip on a condom. Then he pinned her arms over her head and aligned himself with her body. Under the night sky, she lifted her hips to allow him to glide into her depths and once again claim her for his own.

Later, in the quiet stillness inside the grotto, Cameron lay replete once again in Julia's arms. After making love outside on the chaise, they'd spent time playing under the stars in the warm pool. Then, with much laughing and splashing, they'd dipped under the rushing waterfall to enter the hidden grotto. After floating in the sparkling waters of the heated cave, they made love again on the very private bank of the inner lagoon.

Cameron grinned as he lifted his head and kissed her. "You realize you just fulfilled my greatest fantasy, right?"

She laughed. "I love you, Cameron." As soon as the words were out, she gasped and covered her mouth.

Cameron froze. What did she expect him to say? He wasn't about to tell her he loved her. He wouldn't do that to her, knowing it would ruin everything. And just in case he'd thought he might have a chance to live and love like a normal man, Martina's appearance earlier that night had reminded him that things would never change. He would always be a terrible risk.

"Well, I guess I said the wrong thing." Julia stirred away from the warmth of their combined body heat. She grabbed one of the towels stacked nearby and wrapped it around her. Then she stood and looked down at him.

"Wait," he said. "Don't go."

"Why would I stay, Cameron? Look, I didn't mean to say it, but now that I have, I'm not sorry. I'm in love with you. But you've completely closed down. How do you think that makes me feel?" She tightened the towel around her. "I'm going back to the room."

He grabbed her hand. "Julia, I care about you."

"I know you do. But I'm not sure that's enough. Not anymore."

"Julia, I can't…" Hell, what was he supposed to say? He'd told her before, he would never love her. Now she was trying to change the rules, but he couldn't let her. She didn't know the consequences. And what she didn't know could hurt her. He pushed himself up and stood at the side of the pool. "Look, I told you from the beginning that I won't…"

"I know, I know. You don't do love."

Her tone was flippant enough that he grabbed her arm. "That's right, and you should be glad of it. You—"

"Let me guess," she said softly, sadly. "I broke the rules, right?"

He ground his teeth together. "Yeah, you did. We had a deal, remember?"

"I don't remember any deal, Cameron." She removed the towel and tossed it on the rocks, then took the steps one at a time, her glorious, long legs sinking deeper into the water.

"I'll go with you," he said.

"I'd rather be alone for a while."

"Too bad." He slid into the water and grabbed her hand.

"Cameron, I think you've said all there is to say."

"No, I haven't."

Turning to glare at him, she said, "What else is there?"

"Just this." He stared into her eyes because if he looked at her gorgeous breasts, he'd probably begin to whimper and admit something he'd be sorry for later. "I'm glad you're in love with me, Julia."

"What?" Her forehead crinkled in confusion. "Why?"

"Because it'll help our marriage run more smoothly."

Her mouth gaped. "What is that supposed to mean?"

"Just that if you're in love with me, you won't be tempted to give up on our marriage. And that's a good thing for all of us."

"Listen, you arrogant bigheaded fool," she said, and jabbed his chest with her finger. "I was never tempted to leave you, but you're pushing it. And don't for one minute think that I don't know the truth."

"What truth?"

"That you're just as much in love with me as I am with you. You can fight it all you want, deny it all you want, but someday you'll admit I was right. I just hope it won't be too late."

Then she dove under the water and swam away.

# Ten

She was in love with him.

Cameron would never admit it out loud—because he valued his body parts—but he was more than thrilled to hear Julia say she loved him. Yeah, he could see she was a bit annoyed with him, but she would get over it. After all, he reasoned, she was in love with him. Now they could go on from here with an even stronger marriage and a great family life. Maybe someday, they'd give Jake a little brother or sister. Who knew?

Did that make him arrogant, as Julia had

accused him of being? Cameron chuckled as he switched the power level on the hose in order to wash down the cars. It had been two days since they'd returned from Monarch Dunes. Two days since Julia had confessed she was in love with him, then turned around and told him he was arrogant for insisting that this was a good thing.

No, he wasn't arrogant. He was smart. Smart, for recognizing that what Julia wanted most in life was a family. Smart, for deciding that Julia and Jake should live with him and be that family together. And smart, for avoiding the fall into love that had ruined his parents' lives and left Cameron wary of ever getting too close to anyone for fear that it might destroy them.

And if he'd ever had second thoughts about opening his heart and accepting that he might be in love, it had only taken the unexpected and unwanted presence of Martina at the party to remind him why that was a bad idea. Had he honestly thought, way back then, that he was in love with her? She was an empty shell compared to Julia.

But seeing Martina had stirred up other memories as well, ones he truly didn't want to revisit. Memories of the myriad mistakes he'd made in ever thinking he was worthy of love. Memories of Wendy, his high school girlfriend, who had upended the notion of love so badly that it had almost ruined his life.

Cameron turned off the water and reeled in the hose. Then he grabbed a chamois and began to dry off the cars.

No, he thought. Whether she knew it or not, Julia was much better off without his love. She could have his affection, his respect, his admiration. Hell, she could have his body, too. She could have just about anything she wanted, but she would never hear Cameron admit to loving her. Doing so would just lead to another disaster his heart couldn't afford.

It wasn't enough for her. Not anymore.

Julia folded the laundry, then opened the dryer to toss in yet another load. She usually didn't mind these household chores. In fact, she generally enjoyed the quiet simplicity of such uncomplicated tasks. But today, nothing was making her happy.

It had been a week since that night in the grotto, and Cameron was still acting as if nothing had happened, nothing had changed. And maybe nothing had changed—for him. But for Julia, the whole world had shifted.

She had thought it would be enough to go through life married to a considerate husband and a wonderful father for her baby. She had agreed to the wedding, agreed to move into his home. Now she wanted more.

Maybe he was right, maybe it wasn't fair of her to change the rules in midstream. But she couldn't help it anymore. It wasn't just that the rules had changed. It was that Julia herself had changed. She had told him she was in love with him and now she needed him to admit the same.

But he wouldn't. He couldn't. They'd discussed it again last night and she had demanded to know why. What had happened in the past that made him refuse to love her now?

She'd even swallowed her pride and asked him if his feelings had anything to do with that woman she'd met at the formal party. Martina. Was he still in love with her?

Cameron had laughed and brushed off her question, saying only that she was barking up the wrong tree, and left it at that. He wouldn't tell her anything more, wouldn't give her any reason for it.

And now she could actually feel her heart breaking. For herself and for him. And for Jake. All this time, she'd tried to convince herself that it was enough to have a family, an attentive husband, a darling baby. But she'd finally come to the realization that it wasn't enough. She wanted it all. And she deserved it all.

The following Saturday, Adam and Trish threw a small party for a few friends to celebrate their pregnancy. Julia brought homemade breads and dessert and helped Trish with the dinner. Later in the kitchen, she stacked the dessert plates.

"Can I wash the dishes?" Julia asked.

"No, no," Trish said easily, hanging the potholders on their hooks. "Adam and I like to clean up the place by ourselves once our guests go home. It's fun to spend the time together, talking and laughing about the evening and planning our next get-together."

Just then, Adam walked into the kitchen and slipped his arms around Trish's waist. "I missed you. Are you done in here?"

"Yes." Trish beamed at him and he kissed her, then laid his cheek against her head.

Later, on the ride home, she turned to Cameron. "It must be wonderful for you to know your brother Adam is so happy."

Cameron glanced at her sideways as he drove down the highway. "Never really thought about it, but I suppose it's nice."

"Nice?" She laughed. "Cameron, the man is so head over heels in love with his wife, he can't see straight."

Cameron held up his hand. "Okay, I know where this is going and we've been there before. For the last time, I'm telling you that we have a great life together. Why can't you just let it go at that?"

He reached for her hand and squeezed it. It was an affectionate move, meant to reassure her that he cared. But oddly enough, she had to blink back unexpected tears that threatened to fall. She refused to cry, refused to act like more of an idiot than she already was. But was it so idiotic to want all of him? She wanted his heart, not just his name. If that made her a fool, then so be it. At least she would be a fool for love. The thought made her smile all the way home.

But the next day, as she put the breakfast dishes in the dishwasher, she felt her world closing in on her. She had to sit down for a minute as she wondered if she was actually sick or if it was just her heart breaking.

"Good grief," she murmured, standing up with determination. She shut the dishwasher door and turned it on. "When did you become such a drama queen?"

Why couldn't she just let it go? But she couldn't. She'd fallen in love with Cameron and all those strong feelings had wormed their way into her heart. She had to do something about them because she was pretty sure that if she continued to live without love, she would lose herself.

With a sigh, she remembered there was one person in the world she could talk to about her problems. She changed Jake's diaper and got him dressed, then packed him in the car and drove to Sally's house.

"What a nice surprise," Sally said when she opened her front door.

"I hope you don't mind that we stopped by without calling."

"Are you kidding?" she said. "I love it. Come in."

"Thanks."

Sally led the way through her comfortable, stylish living room to her big sunny kitchen. "Don't ever think you can't drop in on me. I love seeing you."

Jake blew bubbles and cooed as he bounced in his carrier.

"Yes, my little darling." Sally tickled his belly. "I love seeing you, too."

She pulled a pitcher of iced tea from the refrigerator, poured two glasses and placed them on napkins on the kitchen table. "Now sit and tell me what's going on. Are you feeling okay? You look a bit down."

Julia shook her hair back and held her shoulders up. "I don't really know where to begin. I suppose I'll start by saying, I'm in love with your son."

"I assume you mean Cameron," Sally said dryly.

Julia choked on her laugh. "Yes, of course."

"Okay, then yes," she said, chuckling. "Of course I know you love him, despite your inability to admit it at the wedding. It makes me so happy to hear you finally say it."

Julia began shredding her napkin. "But he doesn't love me, Sally."

"What?" Frowning, Sally sat back in her chair.

"Honey, of course he does. He loves you very much. I can tell with every look he gives you. I've never seen him so happy."

"Why won't he tell me, then?"

"Tell you what?"

Julia gave Sally a look of frustration. "Why won't he tell me he loves me?"

Sally took a slow sip of her tea. "He's never told you?"

"No," Julia admitted, and buried her face in her hands. "And I feel so stupid, so needy. It's making me sick inside. We actually agreed, when we got married, that love wouldn't come into it."

"You did what?" Sally sounded sincerely shocked.

"Oh, I know what you're thinking," Julia said. "But it seemed like the right thing to do at the time. We married in order to provide Jake with two parents who lived together and loved him. And I was just so happy to be a part of your family, I had to do it."

"Oh, sweetie." She sniffled.

"But now I've fallen in love with Cameron and I've told him, but he insists he's not in love with me. And the thing is, Sally, we're so happy otherwise. So maybe I should just stop whining and be content with what I've got."

Julia sat up straight and looked at her mother-in-law with resolve. "But I can't. I used to think I could be happy without love, but I want it all, Sally. I want him to love me."

"Oh, dear." Sally jumped up from the table and stooped down next to Julia, where she rubbed her arm and patted her cheek. "He does love you, sweetie. Believe me, I know my son. He's not an easy man, but he's worth the battle."

"He really is," Julia said through a light mist of tears.

"Now, you need to stop worrying so much."

"I'm trying."

"Good girl," Sally said. "Now try harder."

Julia laughed, then took hold of Sally's hand and squeezed it. "But I need to ask you something really serious, and I hope you'll keep it between us."

"Anything, sweetie."

Julia bit her lip, then took a deep breath and said what she'd come here to say. "Is there something about Cameron that makes him not want to love me? Oh, that sounds so stupid but I need to know. Is it something about me? Or is it him?"

"Oh, my," Sally said, pushing herself up. She began to pace around the kitchen as she talked. "Poor Cameron. Your question makes me wonder if this whole thing might be because of his father. He was a horrible man. I never got the complete story because the records were sealed, but I knew he was violent. I don't want to alarm you, but I did find out that the man killed Cameron's mother, then killed himself."

"Oh, that's awful. Cameron's never said anything."

"No, he wouldn't. But he was so unhappy when he first came to live with us."

"Oh, God," Julia whispered, as she considered the sad little boy he'd been back then.

"Then, when he was a senior in high school," Sally said, "he met a girl." She told Julia about

Wendy. "He always blamed himself for her horrible behavior."

"But that's not fair," Julia cried.

"No, but that's Cameron. I'll never forget it when he told me it was his fault and that his father was right."

"Oh, dear."

"Maybe I shouldn't have told you all this," Sally said, frowning. "I don't want you to worry that he might hurt you. He wouldn't."

Julia's eyes widened in disbelief, then she started to laugh. "Hurt me? Cameron? He doesn't have a violent bone in his body."

Sally smiled. "It's true. He never was much of a fighter. Oh, sure, he went and joined the marines, but it wasn't because he was looking for a fight. My theory was that his early childhood was so chaotic, he was always seeking more control and order in his life. I think he appreciated that aspect of the military."

Julia made a face. "Well, he certainly likes to control things, doesn't he? But still, he wouldn't hurt a fly. He's the most gentle man I know."

"Yes he is," Sally said, then smiled slyly. "But I'm thinking you might need to ruffle his feathers a bit before he comes to that realization for himself."

Julia frowned at her for a moment, then slowly, understanding dawned. "Oh, Sally, you're a wise woman."

She splayed her hands out. "That's exactly what I keep telling my sons."

Cameron brought her a beautiful butterfly pin made of yellow diamonds and sapphires.

"Oh, Cameron, it's lovely," she said. "But why?"

"No reason."

She took a deep breath. "Are you sure it's not because you're in love with me?"

"Julia…"

"I know, I know." She held up her hand. "It's okay, I know you won't say it. But I do want to make sure of one thing. You love Jake, right?"

"What? Of course I do," he said and stared impatiently out the window.

"I'm glad to hear it, for your sake and Jake's."

"What are you getting at?" he asked.

She placed the lovely pin back in its cushioned jewelry box. She smiled at him and her tone turned blunt. "It'll just make the custody agreement easier to deal with once Jake and I move back to my house."

"Once you—what?" Stunned, he spun her around to face him. "What's that supposed to mean? You're not moving out. We're married. You're not going anywhere."

She clasped her hands together. "I thought it would be enough, Cameron. But it's not. You're a wonderful man, kind and attentive, and so good with Jake. You're an amazing lover and a great friend. But you don't love me, and I want a husband who will love me."

"I'm your husband," he bellowed, then remembered the baby and lowered his voice. "This is all wrong, Julia. You're trying to change the rules again."

"I don't think I am," she said quietly. "I just

think that from now on, I'm following my own rules."

"And what are your rules, Julia?" he said, with just a hint of sarcasm.

"There's only one rule, so far," she said. "I deserve to be loved."

"I can give you almost anything," he bit out, "but I can't give you that."

"Even though I know you love me?"

"You're wrong, babe. I don't love you."

She struggled to catch her breath. He'd never denied it quite that harshly before. But she would get through this. "All right then. I guess that's it."

"I'm sorry," he said, rubbing his neck in frustration. "But you made me angry. Look, I don't want to hurt you. Ever. And that's why…" He stopped.

"That's why…what?" she asked finally.

"That's why I'll never tell you I love you."

She sighed and prayed for patience. "Cameron, you've given me more than fifty thousand dollars worth of jewelry."

"Exactly," he said, as if he were praising a bright six-year-old. "Doesn't that prove that I care about you? Haven't I treated you well and given you things to remind you of our good times together? Can't that be enough?"

"All those things are a sign that you love me," she said pleasantly. "So you might as well just say it."

"Look, I won't do this," he said, pacing the room. "You keep going over this same issue and it's never going to turn out to your satisfaction."

"You're right, and that's why I think we need to separate for a while."

"No." His fists bunched up and he gritted his teeth, seeming to struggle for the words that would stop her from making demands while also explaining why things had to be done his way. Finally, he composed himself enough to speak. "Look, I grew up in a bad place. My father was…"

"Your father?" she prompted after a moment.

"Was a jackass," he said with force. "Violent. Mean. My mother suffered for it."

She winced. "Did he hurt you?"

He laughed without humor. "Once in a while. Didn't mean anything. Mostly he took his rage out on my mother. And that's a fact I'm not exactly proud of."

"Why?"

"I didn't protect her, did I?"

"How old were you?"

He shrugged. "Six, seven. Doesn't matter. I couldn't stop him. But the worst part was that every time he hit her, he would yell that he was doing it because he loved her."

Julia cringed as she finally saw the reason behind Cameron's reluctance to admit love. "That's awful."

"He *loved* her," Cameron repeated, his face a mask of revulsion and pain. "And he showed his *love* by beating the crap out of her."

"Oh, Cameron," she said, and reached out to touch his shoulder in a move meant to comfort him.

He flinched. "No. Don't."

"But—"

"Don't you get it?" He stepped back from her. "I have that same violent streak buried some-where inside me. I know it's there. So I'll never give in. I'll never love. Believe me, I've tried. It didn't work. In fact, it ruined people's lives. I'm a bad risk. Do you understand now?"

"But you're not anything like your father," she said gently.

"It's not that simple." He raked his fingers through his hair. "Look, I know you want to hear the words, but I'll never say them. And I'll never feel them, either. I care about you, Julia, but I refuse to hurt you like my father hurt my mother. I couldn't live with myself if that hap-pened."

Julia would never say it aloud, but she was already hurting. Bleeding. For him. "Do you remember our wedding night?"

He seemed taken aback by her non sequitur. "Of course."

"I was so angry with you."

He grimaced. "Yeah, I know. For good reason."

"I stormed out and you spent the night on the

couch, remember?" she persisted. "I think I hit you at one point."

"You were pissed off."

"But nothing happened."

"Well, sure it did," he said, looking at her as though she'd lost her mind. "The next night we had a great time. You don't remember?"

She rolled her eyes. "Yes, I remember that part. But I'm talking about when I was so angry. I was yelling at you, and I could tell you were angry, too. But you didn't hit me back. And the same thing happened when I painted the kitchen. You were furious with me."

"Yeah, so?"

"Why didn't you hit me?" she persisted.

He frowned. "Look, you're upset right now, but you've got to know that I would never hit you—"

"That's right!" Her eyes lit up. "You would never hit me because you're so *non*violent, it's ridiculous."

"No, that's not why," he muttered, walking

away. "I'll never hit you because I don't love you."

Julia was startled. But then she began to laugh.

"It's true," he said, then turned and pointed at her in warning. "Don't push me, Julia."

Still laughing, she walked right up to him and pushed his chest, hard. He didn't budge. Julia shook her head and wrapped her arms around him, whispering, "I'm pushing you, Cameron, but you would still never hit me. I know you wouldn't. It's not in your makeup."

Resting her head on his chest, she held him tightly and took a moment to mourn the traumatized young boy he used to be. And she felt herself falling more in love with the strong, generous man he was today. The stubborn, ox-headed man who refused to recognize love when it shoved him in the chest.

After a long moment, she lifted her head and gazed at him. "Do you remember when you asked me why I always baked cupcakes?"

"Yeah."

"I told you that after my parents died, whenever

it was my birthday, Cook would give me a cup-cake to celebrate the occasion. What I didn't say was that Cook told me it would be a waste of time and energy to bake an entire cake just for one little girl. So every year, I got that one cupcake."

Her shoulders trembled at the memories and he tightened his hold on her.

"One sad little cupcake with one candle in the middle," she said, and tried to laugh about it. "In my mind, cupcakes began to symbolize my life. And now I can see they symbolized my loneli-ness."

"Oh, baby," he murmured, and rubbed her back.

"Sometimes I would go into the kitchen and beg Cook to let me help with the baking, just to be near another human being in that big old drafty mansion. After a while, I discovered I was really good at baking."

"You're more than good at it."

"Thanks," she said. "I used to bring cupcakes to school sometimes and I saw how they made everyone feel better, especially myself. It was nurturing and fun to bake for other people and it kept some of the loneliness at bay."

She stepped away from Cameron's embrace and looked him in the eye. "It might've been a brilliant business decision to start a bakery that specialized in cupcakes, but now I'm thinking of changing my business plan."

"Yeah?" he said, sounding almost afraid to ask what she had in mind.

"Yeah," she said adamantly. "I'm not going to settle for cupcakes anymore. I want the whole damn cake."

She told him she needed space to think about things, then packed her bags and Jake's baby gear.

Cameron was beyond pissed off that she was leaving and taking Jake with her. "This is absurd, Julia. I don't want you to go."

"You can stop me with a word," she said lightly, though he could see her eyes were bright with tears. "No, make that three words."

He stared at her, his mouth a firm, thin line, saying nothing.

Awash with a sudden wave of grief, she nodded. "That's what I thought." She put Jake into his baby seat. "Say bye-bye to daddy."

Jake bounced in his seat and waved his hands. "Dada!"

Cameron stared after them as they drove down the driveway and disappeared, leaving him with nothing but his famous grip on control.

# Eleven

Barely one hour later, Sally was knocking on his door.

"Come on in, Mom," Cameron said, holding the door open for her. "You want a beer?"

"Of course I don't want a beer," she said, dropping her purse on the living room chair as she followed him into the kitchen. "Cameron, what is going on? You two looked so happy. I was so proud of you for finally accepting love into your life."

"It wasn't what it looked like, Mom." He shrugged. "We had an arrangement."

"Oh, don't be ridiculous," she said, waving his words away. "Arrangements. Good heavens. You kids today."

"Mom, I don't—"

"Look me in the eye and tell me you are not head over heels in love with Julia."

He gritted his teeth and stared her in the eyes. "No."

She narrowed her gaze. "No, you won't tell me or no, you're not in love."

He folded his arms across his chest defiantly. "I'm telling you I'm not in love with her."

She blinked in surprise. "My goodness. Well, I guess I'll be going."

"No need to rush off," he said, a little desperately. "You want to go for a swim or something?"

"No, I got what I came here for."

"Mom," he said, shaking his head. "I'm sorry."

"I am, too, dear," Sally said, and collected her purse as she headed for the front door. "Cameron, you know I love you very much."

"I love you, too, Mom."

"I'm glad, because there's something I need to say to you." She turned and he could read the disappointment in her eyes. "It's been a long time since you lied to me, Cameron Duke, but you're lying now. To me, and to yourself. You are nothing like your father and you know it. Now, I didn't raise a fool, so stop acting like one. You get that wonderful girl and her darling baby back inside this house or heads will roll."

Damn, they didn't call her the Steel Camellia for nothing, Cameron thought ruefully. After his mother left, he took some time to brood for a while. Sally was wrong about the whole lying thing, of course. But he'd been the good son and had allowed her to say what she needed to say.

Now, alone in the house, it almost felt good, necessary even, to wallow in the pain. It had only been a few hours, but he already missed Julia like he would have missed a number of key body parts. More, in fact. Somehow, over the last few months, she had become an essential part of his life, like breathing out and breathing in. So now how was he supposed to live without breathing Julia?

But he would do it. And maybe it was better this way. He'd warned her from the start that he didn't do the whole love thing, and she'd tried to change the rules. She was asking too much, making demands. Cameron Duke didn't work that way. Nobody changed his rules but him.

Still, he missed Julia and Jake like crazy.

He was well into his second beer when the doorbell rang again. He wasn't surprised to see Adam and Brandon let themselves into the house, but he was shocked to see Brandon carrying a small white box with the word Cupcake stenciled in navy blue across the top.

"What are you doing with those?" Cameron asked irately.

"I stopped by Julia's store and bought them," Brandon said with a grin. "Hey, now that you and she are breaking up, I'm thinking she might want to go out sometime." He took a bite of a red-velvet cupcake and moaned, then slid into a dining room chair. "Holy smokes. You let her and these cupcakes get away? Dude, you're nuts. I'm calling her tonight."

Cameron started toward him with both hands fisted. "If you want to live, you'll think twice about that."

Adam grabbed Cameron's arm before he could get any farther. "Don't be a fool."

"Why not?" Cameron asked. "That seems to be the popular opinion of me right now."

"Well, a fool is what you are," Brandon said matter-of-factly, and took another bite of the cupcake.

"And you're a dead man," Cameron said, folding his arms across his chest.

Adam laughed. "Look at you."

Cameron glanced down at himself, then snarled at his brother. "What?"

"You're standing there making threats, but we all know you would never hurt Brandon."

"Don't count on it," Cameron muttered.

Adam shook his head. "Even when we were kids, you never threw the first punch. Ever."

"True enough," Brandon said with a shrug.

"Whereas, Brandon used to get into fights all the time," Adam grinned. "Remember?"

Brandon smiled at the memories, then glanced at Cameron. "You never fought about anything unless some kid hit you first. Even then, you'd do whatever you could to prevent another punch."

"Yeah, always the diplomat," Adam said. "I only remember one time when you were actually forced to defend yourself."

"Yeah," Brandon said, then laughed. "And that was only because Jerry Miles was going to beat the crap out of me."

"I should've let him."

"But you didn't," Adam said pointedly. "You entered that fight with grim resignation. There was never any blood lust with you. You never enjoyed it, never got into it. And you never will."

"Yeah," he muttered. "Maybe."

"No, not maybe," Adam shot back. "Don't you get it? You're not a fighter. You're not violent. You're nothing like your old man and you never will be."

* * *

That Saturday, Sally brought Jake over to Cameron's house so he could spend the day with his daddy. Julia had an emergency at the bakery, Sally explained, so she had agreed to bring Jake by.

That's when it really hit him how much he missed Julia, more than he'd ever thought possible. So much that it hurt him physically.

He took Jake swimming in the pool. After some serious splashing and laughing, they got out and Cameron dried Jake off. He let him crawl in the thick grass of the yard while Cameron quickly dried himself off. Then he watched in amazement as Jake crawled to the fence and used it to lever himself up off the ground. He stood all by himself in the grass and took his first step.

"Dada!" Jake cried, then plopped back down on his butt. He laughed and Cameron swooped him up with delight.

"Jake, what did you do?" Cameron asked, astounded by his son's ability. "Can you do that again? Can you walk by yourself like a big boy? Here, I'll help you."

Cameron steadied Jake, who stood where he was for a few seconds, then took a tentative step. He began to wobble and finally fell on his knees. This time, he screamed bloody murder. Cameron picked him up to comfort him.

"That's okay, buddy," he crooned as he hugged the little guy. "We'll just kiss it and make it better. All better."

Jake shuddered and sniffled as Cameron soothed away his pain.

"Hey, you're getting to be a real big boy," he murmured, patting his back. "Come on. It's all better now. All better. And just wait till your mama hears what you did."

The emotion hit him so fast and hard, Cameron almost fell to his knees himself. Julia needed to know that Jake had walked. He raced into the house to call her immediately. Who better to share this special moment with?

As Cameron picked up the phone, he rubbed his chest, recognizing the heavy feeling. He'd felt it that night at the big party, while watching Julia as she talked to his friend Byron. Now the feelings seemed to come in waves and they filled his chest with so much warmth, he had a hard time catching his breath. It wasn't pain. It was an emotion he'd never felt with any other woman but her.

He stared at the phone for a few seconds, then put it back in its cradle. What would he do when Jake had another special moment? Would he rush to call Julia? And what would happen when Jake started walking for real? If Cameron wasn't there, would Julia call him to describe his every movement, bit by bit, over the phone? Was Cameron prepared to miss all those special moments of their lives?

And what would happen if Jake fell down again? What if Cameron wasn't there when Jake cried? Who would kiss and make it better?

And what if something happened to Julia? Who would kiss her and make her feel better when she was hurt? She'd spent much of her life having no one around to do that for her. He was ashamed to admit that he hadn't come forward to do it for her, either.

Would she find someone else? Someone with the guts to stand by her side and love her as she deserved to be loved? Would some other man move into Julia's life and take Cameron's place?

Would Cameron really sit on the sidelines and let that happen?

"Hell, no," he swore. If anyone was going to love Julia, it was going to be him.

"Damn it, Julia," he muttered, grabbing his keys and Jake's diaper bag. "I warned you."

He drove up into the hills above Dunsmuir Bay to Glen Haven Farm, Julia's home. She and Jake had their living quarters in the east wing. It was a nice set-up, with three bedrooms, a couple of bathrooms, a good-size sitting room, as Julia called it, and a great old kitchen. It was comfy and lived-in, unlike the rest of the big old house.

He still couldn't picture the little girl she'd been, trying to grow up in what was more like a fine arts museum than a home. But that was okay, because he was determined to make sure she wouldn't live here much longer.

Holding Jake securely in his arms, Cameron rang the doorbell and waited for the maid or housekeeper to open the heavy double doors.

Instead, Julia showed up, looking beautiful and sexy in jeans, sneakers and an apron spotted with chocolate smears. "Hi."

"Hi," Cameron said, and gazed into the dark blue eyes he'd fallen for the first time he ever saw her. He'd settled on a plan of action on the drive over here. He'd worked out all the right things to say, and just how to say them. But when faced with his fate, he simply blurted, "I love you, Julia. Please come home."

He watched her swallow, then she bit her lip as her forehead furrowed in a frown. "I'm sorry. I'm not sure I heard you quite right. Could you maybe repeat that three or four more times?"

"I'm in love with you, Julia," he said. "I love you more than anything in the world. I want you and Jake to live with me and I want more babies and I want a dog. A big one. But more than anything else, I want you back, Julia. I love you so much. Come back home and don't ever leave me again."

She tilted her head. "Once more?"

He laughed and grabbed her in a fierce embrace and she kissed him with all the love she could muster. "Of course I'll come home. I've just been waiting for you to ask."

"Mama!" Jake giggled and waved his hands.

Cameron's heart was bursting with joy. "I love you more than anything. Will you marry me all over again? We'll have a huge, fancy wedding. You can wear a designer dress and we'll invite a thousand people. There'll be a gigantic cake. I promise we'll do it the right way this time. Just please come home with me. I love you."

She kissed him again with her arms still wrapped around him and Jake. "Silly man. You still don't get it. I don't need another wedding, Cameron. I already have everything I've ever wanted right here in my arms."

\* \* \* \* \*

*Discover Pure Reading Pleasure with*

## Visit the Mills & Boon website for all the latest in romance

**Buy** all the latest releases, backlist and eBooks

**Find out** more about our authors and their books

**Join** our community and chat to authors and other readers

**Free** online reads from your favourite authors

**Win** with our fantastic online competitions

**Sign** up for our free monthly eNewsletter

**Tell us** what you think by signing up to our reader panel

**Rate** and review books with our star system

# www.millsandboon.co.uk

 Follow us at twitter.com/millsandboonuk

 Become a fan at facebook.com/romancehq